SHIFTING SIDES

DANIELLE FORREST

The Eternal Scribe Publishing
Indianapolis, IN

PROLOGUE

The hunters fanned out over the field, weapons at the ready. They knew what was at stake. Behind them, their city stood as a constant reminder. Behind them, their families were starving. Behind them, people were dying.

All because of these stupid vermin.

They walked through fields that once fed thousands. The food was gone, eaten. They were running out of options. The little bastards seemed to reproduce as quickly as they killed them.

They'd kept them out of the city, at least. It was little consolation, though. The king had sent reinforcements, sent resources from other cities. But with the Tannar long dead, no beasts could carry loads large enough to feed an entire city, not if they needed to keep those loads safe from the creatures that had laid siege to their home.

His feet crunched through the broken plants, hands squeezing and relaxing on his weapons as they moved forward in a line.

He constantly reminded himself to keep his muscles relaxed. Usually, it wasn't an issue, but usually, he didn't have this much on his shoulders. As a hunter working for the city, he eliminated wayward predators or the odd creature eating their crops. In his free time, he killed animals to help feed his family and sold what they couldn't use. It wasn't easy, but it was rewarding.

It certainly wasn't this stressful.

Something moved, shifting some flattened, dying vegetation, and he pounced, swinging out with his blade. It lodged hard into the earth, jarring his arm, but a creature squealed, flailing and dislodging the crops hiding it. The men and women around him tensed, wanting to join in, but they couldn't. They couldn't break rank.

Break rank, and the city would be lost.

He pulled back and swung again. With a final squeak, it stopped moving. Blood dripped from the tip of his long blade as he pulled it from the ground. He glanced to each side of him and smiled, but the expression didn't reach his eyes.

Then someone screamed. He tensed again, lifting his weapon, and his mouth dropped.

A swarm of them, small and deadly, surged toward them, slipping out of the field they'd decimated. He caught motion in his peripheral vision, and he swung as the beasts reached their line. It sounded like a battle erupted as the blade connected, sending the little monster flying through the air.

Then the tempo of the fight changed. The screams increased. Someone yelled, "Run!"

He looked up and around him. More than half the hunters had fallen. Most were running, and it looked like a sea of brown bodies were flooding toward them.

We've lost.

CHAPTER ONE

DAY 1

"*H*appy Christmas," Emma said to the empty control room as she looked at the planet that would soon be home, at least for the next couple years. It looked a lot like Earth from orbit, but it had just enough differences to make it feel… wrong. Too much uninterrupted water. Landmasses in the wrong places. Uncanny Valley, that was the term used in robotics for this feeling.

Still, they'd traveled here for a reason. They had a mission, and she was excited to see it through. The phrase she'd once heard on Doctor Who never seemed more apropos: "Halfway through the dark." They'd arrived, but the battle had yet to begin.

By the Earth calendar they'd continued to use, it had just chimed midnight on Christmas Eve. It would be the longest Christmas Eve and Christmas ever since the planet they were about to set foot on had 72 hour days. But the atmosphere, temperature, and other essential elements all resembled Earth. At least, that was what the scientists had said.

Emma had just piloted the mission. Most people here looked down on her. At least, everyone but the children. The children all marveled at her controls, trying to press buttons and touch displays. They took turns playing at pilot, and she sat back with a smile, knowing they couldn't harm anything without the codes.

She loved children, but the life she'd chosen didn't exactly lend to having any herself. She'd known that going in, had accepted it. Even so, this mission was making her seriously rethink her chosen career. She loved flying, loved spaceships, but she was looking forward to the upcoming mission.

They would live on this planet for a couple years before she and the crew returned for Earth. She'd thought it would be fun, an adventure. They would be living in a tight-knit settler community. They would be building something. In a way, it reminded her of growing up on her parents' farm, which was part of the reason her CO had chosen her for this mission. With her agricultural experience, engineering degree, and pilot credentials, she was the perfect pick.

Unfortunately, the people here didn't see it that way. They didn't like her. The parents shooed their children away when they caught them playing in the control room. They scowled at her, making their disdain for her obvious. To them, Emma was a necessary evil made obsolete once they landed. After all, what use was a pilot once they settled planet-side?

Emma chose not to think about their cold looks and snide comments. Her career and childhood had left her damn close to an expert in construction, farming, and repairing technology. She *knew* she would be useful, even if they refused to accept it. They just saw her as a hotshot pilot that would be about as useful as tits on a bull once they landed. They didn't know or care that she'd never been the wild type, that she'd never fit in with the other pilots. She'd never played it fast and loose, never slept around. In fact, after years of finding no one attractive, she'd finally figured she was probably asexual and moved on. It had made her an outsider, but she tried not to let it get her down. That was only one part of her life, a part she didn't *need* to be happy. She preferred to look at the bright side, setting her sights on a goal and steamrolling toward it.

Unfortunately, her unending good cheer and determination had been tested to its limits on the trip to HD 85512 b. Humanity had discovered the planet in the early 21st century, but had only recently concluded that it could sustain human life.

Emma opened the intercom. "Happy Christmas, ladies and gents. We are about to start our descent to HD 85512 b. Please secure all items and strap yourselves into your appropriate seating. Descent will begin in ten minutes."

And now for the waiting.

"Alright, loves. It's time for our final descent. Make certain your harnesses are secured, and we will commence shortly." Emma had spent the last ten minutes orbiting the planet, the computer scanning potential landing sites. Now, she inputted the chosen coordinates, calculated the trajectory, and let the computer plot the smoothest course. The SmartGlass popped up a glowing green line that stretched across her view of the planet and space, indicating the path she should take. Blue water and white clouds served as backdrop, with the black of space framing it.

With a few finger swipes and a push of the control sticks, she moved them forward, following the calculated path. Resistance increased as the *Endeavour* entered the planet's atmosphere, and its gravitational pull tried to draw them down. A red hue built across the SmartGlass while a gentle vibration hummed through her wherever she connected with the ship. While the gravity proved stronger than she'd expected, the engines did their job, responding with alacrity. But at more than three times Earth's size, the forces surprised her, and she had to remind herself to pull up more.

They passed through white, puffy clouds, and the planet stretched out before her—big blue oceans sprinkled with smaller islands and a single large continent they would soon land on. "Brilliant," she said, reverence in her voice and emotion nearly choking her. She watched the continent below, marveling at the untouched beauty of it. No roads, lights, buildings. Just a cross-shaped mountain range running through its center and purple vegetation as far as the eye could see. It almost felt wrong to land there, to contaminate it with their presence. After all, they would only destroy it. It was what humans did.

Emma passed the continent, nearly never-ending blue flying by underneath her. She would pass the continent six more times before they could land. This planet had a lot more water than Earth did. "I wonder if it's salt or fresh water." Probably salt water, just like on Earth.

Another few passes and the excitement inside her grew to the point of bursting. A grin graced her face, and that all too familiar exhilaration surged through her once more. She should have been a fighter pilot, she supposed, because she could *live* for this feeling. But she chose to join NASA rather than NSS or even Air Force.

The SmartGlass's red tint from reentry faded as the ship slowed. Emma resisted the urge to hold her breath as she approached the landing site. She slowed the ship, adjusting the angle of descent, and activated the vertical thrusters. The thrusters roared as they tried to keep the ship airborne. They hovered in the air for a moment, then sank to the ground with a soft thud. Perfect landing.

"We've landed on HD 85512 b. You may now unfasten your harnesses and move about the ship once more." Emma ended the broadcast and popped the clasp on her own harness, flipping the straps over her head. Outside the SmartGlass, a truly alien world greeted her. Green grasses tipped in blue pollen swayed in a breeze in the large meadow they'd landed in while trees with almost black bark and a canopy of bright purple foliage stood in the periphery. A lopsided grin crossed her face, and she laughed. "Oh, this is going to be fun."

CHAPTER TWO

Emma pushed out of her seat, her hand gliding over the smooth console as she about-faced, aiming for the locker next to her bunk. She popped it open, grabbing a small, black bag she clipped to her waist before rushing to the door. She hit the door controls, stepping forward without thinking or seeing.

A sea of passengers and crew surged around her, slamming into her and shoving her out of the way in their haste to step on the planet's surface. Emma frowned, but otherwise didn't let her ire show. She didn't want it to taint her good mood. The sound of dozens of excited voices echoed off the walls of the metal hallways, making her cringe. She moved out of the main hall, standing in the doorway to the control room, while the others rushed past. It wasn't worth the struggle.

A little girl in bright blue overalls stopped and stared up at her, reaching for Emma with her hand. Emma glanced down and took the little, sticky appendage in her own, pulling the girl out of harm's way before she got trampled.

"I'll wait with you," the little girl said before sticking her thumb in her mouth.

Emma smiled, instantly enamored with her. "I would be delighted for the company, sweetling."

The girl smiled around her thumb, then sidled up closer to Emma, nearly hugging her leg. Emma ran her hand over the girl's head. She's seen her before, but the girl had spoken more in the last few minutes than the entire trip. She always came with the other kids, but never engaged, always standing apart, sucking her thumb and looking ready to bolt.

They watched the people rush by together. Emma couldn't help wondering about the girl's parents. Where were they? The USS *Endeavour* wasn't that big of a ship. Countless ships, even much older ships, boasted crews in the hundreds, but the *Endeavour* only housed about fifty. Big enough to be unwieldy, but not so big she shouldn't know everyone on board after a few months. That is, if everyone was willing.

The crowd thinned, then Emma and the little girl slipped in behind the flow of people. They stood in silence as they breached the exterior door. Emma stood there, jaw slack, speechless and awed. Another world. New trees. New dirt. New air. New everything.

Emma looked down at the girl only to see her hand limp at her side, thumb forgotten. "It's beautiful, isn't it?"

The girl nodded slowly.

Emma tugged on their joined hand. "Come. Let's get a closer look."

The girl nodded again, and Emma led them down the steps and onto that new soil. Conversation surrounded them in a constant white noise, while a sweet scent she couldn't identify filled the air. She'd picked a large section of relatively empty, flat land. Long green and blue vegetation littered the meadow, but nothing else until one reached the tree line, where the trees stood tall and thick, undisturbed for centuries. Each tree sprouted purple blossoms and leaves of the same green and blue as the vegetation in the meadow. She hadn't noticed the leaves from the control room. *I wonder why the bark is purple, though.* "Curious."

A loud noise, like the roar of some great beast, cut through the air. Beeyun froze, a slice of fear rippling through him.

You're not brave. See how you freeze?

The voice, a voice in his head that had taunted him his entire life, snapped him out of his shock. He would never be a leader, but he could try to fulfill this role and be the person his people needed. Beeyun tried harder than anyone else he'd ever met, would push himself beyond the breaking point if necessary, and today would be no different. He tipped his head back, searching for the source of that sound, but caught nothing. He'd never heard anything like it on Ara before, and he didn't care to ever again, either. It didn't bode well, of that he was certain. Unease settled in his gut.

Beeyun shoved the feeling aside, but nagging impressions remained. Half-formed thoughts of invasions and dangerous beasts danced along the edges of his psyche. He'd only caught a glimpse of the great sky beast before it disappeared, hidden by the trees that limited his view of the sky above. Certainly, he hadn't seen enough to evaluate the threat, know what he was dealing with. He continued to run in the direction it was heading.

The noise didn't cease, at least not at first. The roar continued, giving him an easy direction to follow. He was determined to find it and protect his territory if necessary. It was his duty, his responsibility to the Danaus, and he refused to fail. The roar stopped, and he skidded to a halt, eyes closed, listening for signs. A hissing sound like an animal's threat display. He followed the hissing, which grew fainter even though he felt certain he was drawing closer. Just a little farther.

He stopped at the tree line, trying to blend in. A large, metal monstrosity sat on the edge of the meadow, looming ominously in the glittering sunlight. People in various shades of brown skin spread out from the metal thing, trespassing on his domain. Beeyun frowned, just *knowing* he had his work cut out for him. They looked like they intended to stay.

But why did they come?

And what did they want?

———

Emma stood on the ground, scanning the tree line for dangers. She might not be NSS, but she knew foreign worlds often held dangers they couldn't predict. Her mind kept coming back to the same question. Why were the tree trunks purple? Emma just *knew* it had significance, but didn't have enough information. She wasn't a scientist, after all.

Instead, she looked for Captain West, the leader of this little expedition. As she scanned the noisy crowd, she registered movement out of the corner of her eye. Emma jerked her head in that direction, releasing the girl's hand and walking forward. She squinted, trying to spot what she'd seen just a moment before.

"Ah! Ah!" the little girl cried out.

Emma spun and grabbed her clammy hand. "Sorry, love. Didn't mean to abandon you there."

The girl leaned into her, letting out a sigh.

"West!" Emma said when she finally caught sight of him.

The captain turned and sighed when he saw who'd spoken. He walked to her and let his exasperation show. "What is it, pilot?"

She tried to let the fact he hadn't bothered to learn her name slip, but it niggled at the back of her mind. They wouldn't even be here if it weren't for Emma. She took a deep breath, shoring up her confidence. "I saw movement along the edge of the meadow, sir. We should move back to the *Endeavour* until security creates a proper protective barrier."

"And who are you to make these suggestions? You're just a pilot."

She breathed through her nose to release the frustration. "That may very well be true. I may be a NASA pilot, but that also means that I trained hand in hand with NSS. One picks things up, even pilots like myself."

He frowned, his expression relenting a little. "You're sure you saw something?"

"Positive." It was in her peripheral vision, and she wasn't sure *what* she saw, but she saw it. "I only want the safety of the people on this mission, sir."

He nodded and waved his hand over his head. "Alright, everyone. Back to the ship. Security, let's do a perimeter sweep and set up a sensor grid."

All but the half-dozen security personnel started filing back into the ship. She could tell the scientists in the group—they were grumbling as they shuffled along.

Emma looked back at the trees, half expecting some native creature to jump out at them, but didn't see any further movement. Maybe she'd imagined it.

But a sick feeling in her chest told her maybe they shouldn't have come.

CHAPTER THREE

*E*mma looked out through the SmartGlass, tapping her fingers against the console, watching the security personnel as they jammed sensors into the ground.

"Knock, knock," West said from behind her.

"Good day, Captain. How can I help you?"

"We need the bay doors opened."

"Right away, Captain." Emma saluted him and stretched to the side a bit, touching the console that controlled the outer doors and airlocks. She typed the four-digit code for the bay doors and selected the "Open" button. "You're good to go, Captain."

"Thank you." He turned and left her on her own again.

She shook her head. They would all be goners without her, but did they appreciate that? No. Captain West couldn't even operate the bay doors.

Not a single person on the ship knew the codes required to operate its systems. It functioned on an antiquated operating system designed for sensitive missions. Only certain people, mainly pilots, knew the various codes. Emma had trained on this type of ship, so the codes were still fresh on her mind. Command chose it because they stopped building non-military ships this small decades ago, and they hadn't scuttled this class of spaceships yet because it still had its uses.

She wiped her hands on the rough material of her pants and got up. "I should lend a helping hand."

Outside, rovers were moving building supplies into the clearing—the first steps toward settlement.

Emma jogged away from the control room and down the main hallway, her steps clapping and echoing off the walls, then into the storage bay. Releasing a breath to recover from the run, she said, "Anybody need a hand?"

Everyone looked up, but nobody asked for help. She tapped her thigh, wondering what she should do. She couldn't just do nothing. So she shrugged it off and stepped into the fray, starting with helping a scientist load a medium-sized, but heavy, box onto a rover.

"Hey, hands off," the woman shrieked, startling Emma. "This thing's fragile. You'll break it."

Emma glared at the woman and shook her head, recognizing the emblem and writing on the box—a Real Time Genotyper. It could test an entire field of crops in a matter of minutes to verify the identity of the plants in question.

It had been developed after the big "GMO" scandal ages ago. People had flipped out when they heard non-GMO crops only had to be 85% GMO-free for the government to flag them that way. The original had taken hours, but the latest models only took minutes and could use raw plant material, rather than requiring the extraction of DNA from the plants first. Her parents had one of the more recent models on their farm.

Instead of arguing with the woman about the instrument's durability, Emma walked away. It just wasn't worth getting upset over.

Emma scanned the room for a non-scientist, hoping to have better luck there. She walked up to a couple women loading building materials onto an almost empty rover. "Mind if I help?"

"Oh, um, what's your name?" the woman asked, her soft voice almost disappearing in the din of the cargo bay.

She sighed. "It's Emma."

"Right. Emma. I'm so terrible with names."

"And you're… Tracy?"

"Close. Lacy."

"Jesus, I'm sorry. I imagine I'm not much better myself."

Lacy waved it off. "It's alright. I didn't see you around a lot."

Emma shrugged. "I'm the pilot."

"Ah, that makes sense. You were doing important piloting things."

She smiled, liking the woman already. Actually, Lacy was the only person who hadn't treated her like shit so far, barring children. "That I was. Now, you need to move these onto the rovers?"

"Yeah. I don't understand why we didn't just load them on when we packed them up in here." She waved her hands, exasperated.

"Couldn't. The rovers are great at traveling over unstable terrain, but takeoff and landing are rough. If we'd loaded them, they would have tipped over. This would have been a bloody mess."

"I like your accent," a girl said.

Emma glanced down at the little girl, recognizing her from the hallway earlier.

Lacy smiled. "That's my daughter, Jacie."

Emma leaned forward. "Why thank you, Jacie. It's a pleasure to make your acquaintance."

The girl laughed—the sound bubbling out of her and lighting up the room like sunshine—then glanced up at her mom. "She's funny."

Emma smiled, marveling at the difference. The girl seemed far more animated in the isolated corner of the cargo bay.

Lacy scrubbed her daughter's messy hair. "Yes, sweetie. She's hilarious. Now, go sit with the other children."

"Yes, mom," Jacie said, but she didn't look overly enthusiastic, slumping her shoulders and shuffling along as slowly as possible.

"You don't see a lot of Brits in NASA," Lacy said, drawing Emma's attention once again.

"Well, my mum's British, but I was born in the US. I just learned to speak from her." She really didn't have *much* of an accent anymore. She'd picked up plenty of American slang when she went off to college and pilot training, but being homeschooled by her mom had certainly affected her speech patterns.

"Ah. Well, it is a very nice accent."

"Thank you."

"Alright, ladies, let's get to work," a woman next to Lacy said.

"And this slave driver," Lacy said, elbowing the woman next to her, "is my wife, Rickelle."

"Rick." Rickelle shrugged, rolling her eyes as she gave Emma a nod in greeting.

"Nice to meet you." Emma pushed up her sleeves and reached for the first beam, lifting it off the pile with Lacy and Rick's help before lowering it onto the rover.

Lacy sighed as they sat on one of the beams in the meadow, drinking from her cup. "This is one hell of a long Christmas Eve."

They'd been working for hours and Emma felt the strain in every muscle, encouraging her to never stand again. They still had hours more before they called it quits for the day. It felt like years since they'd landed, like it was some faraway dream, but it hadn't even been a full day.

"Not exactly like putting up the tree, is it?" Emma felt more at ease. The sensors lining the hull flashed in her peripheral vision. Security was alert, and the perimeter sensor grid was in place, but she still felt like they weren't alone, like something was out there.

"Did you know that this planet has 72 hour days?" Rick said, leaning in to kiss her wife.

"Yes, Rick," Emma and Lacy said in unison before bursting into giggles.

Rick shook her head at their antics, brought on by their brutally long work day. "It's like someone's cloned my wife or something."

"Now take that back. I look nothing like your wife."

"Yeah, I'm way prettier," Lacy chimed in.

They burst into another fit of exhaustion-fueled giggles as Rick shook her head again and walked away.

Emma let out a deep breath. "You were messing with her head, weren't you?"

"All the time. It's the secret to a good marriage. Gotta keep her on her toes."

"Oh, she's got her hands full with you." Emma shook her head, her face hurting from smiling so much.

"Yes, but I'm worth it."

Emma tried not to let her smile fall, but talking about relationships always made her a little depressed. She reinforced her flagging smile and changed the subject. "So, why did you guys join this mission? I mean, the scientists I get. It's the colonists that baffle me a bit."

"Well, isn't it the same for you?"

Emma shrugged. "Maybe. Maybe not. I think the longer I'm on this mission, the more I second guess myself. I'm mean, why did I even come at all?" Not that she'd had a choice. Her CO had given her the assignment, but with the caveat that she could decline it since it was such a long deployment. Still, she'd only recently graduated pilot training. How could she have refused?

"Well, I'm glad you did."

"Thank you."

"So, why *did* you come, Emma?"

Emma paused, uncertain how to proceed. Why did she? Sure, her CO had given it to her, but she'd actually looked forward to it. "It kind of feels like an adventure, I guess. Trying something new? Maybe a little playing house." She laughed.

Lacy nodded. "Makes sense. For us, it's a fresh start. You look around Earth, and it's all concrete and buildings. It feels cold, oppressive, alienating. This is a chance at a new start. And an adventure, like you said. Exploring a new world. Who'da thunk it?"

"Yes, indeed." Emma stood up. "Well, we'd better get back to work."

"Yeah. Lot more to do before the sun sets."

Emma worked longer and harder than anyone else. She couldn't really say what drove her. Maybe a desire to see the mission succeed? After most everyone had gone to their beds, she continued on, stopping occasionally to look into the trees. "Paranoia, Emma. It's just paranoia."

But something about the forests surrounding her left her uneasy, anxious, like sensing a predator on the wind and waiting for it to strike. That was ludicrous, though, wasn't it? After all, there wasn't a predator on Earth they hadn't conquered. And they had security forces here, weapons. They were fine, safe.

Weren't they?

She rubbed her hands on her pants again, choosing to ignore the blisters forming there, but the stinging pain was a constant, nagging passenger in her mind.

They'll heal.

Earlier in the day, they'd finished the initial stages of construction, which required a minimum of two people. They couldn't lift the framework beams any other way. But after the frames were up, a single person could continue as long as he or she wanted. And Emma had made the most of that.

She smiled at her progress. Prefab buildings like these went up fast and easy, and they were all the same. Consisting almost entirely of beams and sheets of metal, a usable shelter could be ready in hours, even for the biggest of buildings. And with the various buildings they'd put up on her parents' farm, she could do this in her sleep. In fact, she felt almost as if she *was* asleep. And as if to emphasize the point, she dropped a sheet of metal siding on her foot and yelped.

"Bloody hell! Gah!" She pranced around, trying to get the feeling back into her right foot. As the throbbing pain subsided enough to allow her to put weight on it again, she sighed. "Okay, I think it's time to stop."

At first, Beeyun didn't know what to do. They were like nothing he'd ever seen before. While similar in form to the Danaus, their skin was adapted to another environment. They wore clothes that were both similar and alien at once. Their technology was strange and alarming to him, but some part of him hoped they would leave soon. Maybe they'd had some equipment that needed repairs. Or maybe they didn't intend any harm. Maybe they were like his people, and they would come to live harmoniously side by side.

But after observing them, he knew better.

Beeyun continued to watch in horror as the aliens built building after building. He'd seen buildings in the cities, enormous edifices that blended in with the environment or emulated natural structures, but nothing like these. Each construct was just as bright and shiny as the beast standing sentinel on the edge of the meadow. Voices he couldn't yet comprehend chatted as they worked, helping each other lift materials or fasten them in place. As he watched, hours passed, and one building after the next received walls, roofs, doors. With technology like this, these people could destroy his entire world in a matter of weeks.

He ground his hands into the bark of the tree at his side, using it to control his emotion, to keep himself still, to just *observe*. His impulses told him to send them packing, but even *he* knew this lot would not be so easily thwarted. They were intelligent beings, not wild animals scared off by a larger predator. He needed to be *smart*. He needed a *plan*.

And the entire time he watched, the sweet scent of maenu teased his senses, keeping him a safe distance from the meadow. The beast landing had disrupted the field, sending the pollen into the air, and all the movement and construction continued to disturb it, leaving Beeyun hesitant to approach any closer.

Time passed and little by little they returned to their massive metal thing—all but one of them. The last one stayed behind, pushing herself well past exhaustion. She just kept going, finishing one building after the next, Beeyun was both horri-fied and in awe of her work ethic and speed. She was clearly strong, accomplished, a being to be respected. He imagined she must be a leader of some kind.

When the sun had just started to approach the trees, she dropped something on her foot and started yelping and jumping around, clearly hurt. Every instinct screamed at him to race into the field and help her, but he stopped himself. No, she was an enemy, trespassing on his land, destroying the natural world his kind loved so much.

She limped off into the metal beast, and he slipped from the trees, breathing carefully to minimize his exposure to the pollen.

Time to get to work.

CHAPTER FOUR

DAY 2

*E*mma woke to screams. She jerked upright, slammed her head into the bulkhead, and fell out of her bunk. "Bloody hell." She held her head, rolling on the floor, praying for the throbbing to go away.

After a few moments, the pain dwindled, and she could release her forehead and open her eyes. She touched the spot gently and looked at her fingertips. "No blood. Well, at least there's that." She wiggled her toes. "And my foot doesn't hurt as much. The beauties of gating, I guess."

Emma stood carefully, her head screaming at her with the slightest movement. The trek to the hallway went on forever. Every step required focus and a degree of finesse she didn't have. Every muscle screamed from the overexertion of the previous day. She didn't even *see* the control room as she crossed it. Arriving at the hallway had her slumping against the doorframe in relief, the metal digging into her side. She frowned. Not a soul walked the halls. Pristine sheet metal walls continued as far as the eye could see in either direction.

She turned right, walked outside, and halted at the top of the steps. "Good Lord. What happened?" Even in the fading light, she could clearly see the destruction. Nothing remained of the work they'd accomplished yesterday. Many of the beams still survived, but the doors… the walls… "What happened?" Her mind couldn't process it for a while.

Claw marks.

That incongruous thought popped into her head, but her eyes narrowed on a piece of metal siding still attached to one of the buildings. The edge had been shredded by what looked like an animal's claws. Around the clearing, people milled about, walking between pieces of metal too small to be useful anymore, the edges ragged from being torn from their moorings.

A man nearby spoke, probably too shell shocked to give her the stink eye as he normally would. "We don't know. All the sensors were active. Something ran straight past them without triggering them and tore the entire place to shreds."

"What?" Emma shook herself out of her reverie, staring at the man who spoke up.

He didn't look at her, and she couldn't make out any details of his appearance as the sun stretched toward the horizon behind him, casting him in silhouette. He shook his head. "So much destruction."

Emma looked back at the damage and whimpered, collapsing to sit on the stairs. It was so unfair. She'd worked so hard yesterday. Tears pricked at her eyes as she scanned the wreckage. "But I got so much done." She'd felt certain everyone would have praised her in the morning, grateful for her efforts, but it was all for nothing.

"What?" he said, finally looking at her.

Emma shrugged. It didn't matter, anyway. She just wanted to crawl back to the control room and curl up in a ball. Words slipped out without conscious thought, not seeing, not hearing, just zoning out as the situation became too much for her exhausted state. "I've always functioned on longer circadian rhythms, so staying up later didn't seem like a hardship. I wanted to get a few more buildings done before heading off to bed."

He raised his eyebrows, then turned to the installation. "There are roofs and siding on a half dozen buildings that were barely started when we went to bed. How much did you get done?"

"Doesn't matter, does it?" The tears threatened with renewed vigor.

"I suppose not, but thank you anyway for your hard work."

"Oh, no problem." Emma smiled, but it didn't reach her eyes. A hysterical chuckle bubbled at the back of her throat, but she forced herself to focus, looking at the clearing with a more critical eye. "Do you think we have the resources to rebuild all of them?"

He scratched his chin, rotating his head back and forth. "We won't be able to build as many buildings. We'll probably end up using native materials to make up the difference."

Emma stood and crossed to the nearest damaged building, stepping over small chunks of metal. She ran a finger along the gouges. "What could do this?" She touched the four jagged tears running in parallel lines. "It almost looks like an animal ripped at it with its claws."

He shrugged. "Maybe one did. You said you saw something yesterday in the woods."

Emma turned around, surprised he'd heard her the day before. She didn't recognize him, didn't know him. She returned to the building, to the damage. "Yeah, but… this?" She shook her head. "This is… I-I don't know. This is beyond anything I could have imagined or feared. What if someone had been out here when this happened? They could have been killed." She ran her hand over the rough edges once more, careful not to cut herself.

"Fortunately, everyone was inside."

Or was it? She looked over at the trees, her hand stilling on the ruptured metal siding. Was it just chance? Or had it waited until everyone was inside before destroying their progress?

They all worked side by side trying to repair the damage. Most of the destruction affected the exterior siding, so they spent the morning organizing supplies while the engineers redesigned the settlement, going from several smaller buildings to one large one. It would require less surface area to pull off.

As the day waxed on, the sun set. The dark presented its own challenges. The planet didn't have a moon, so they made do with lamps. Emma had turned on the ship's external lights, which were usually used to guide it to the ground during night landings or emergency situations. All combined, they had enough light to work by, but it didn't stop Emma from squinting.

Or from sinister shadows teasing her senses, causing her to flinch at regular intervals. It didn't help that there was the constant sound of metal being thrown about, wobbling and banging as they worked.

"Bloody hell," she said, jumping around and cursing as she held her hand.

"What happened, Emma?" Lacy said, following her like a mother hen, her hands reaching out for her friend.

"Being bloody stupid." She held her hand tight, the lack of circulation making it feel a wee bit better. Oh, Emma was terrible with hammers. One would think humanity could have invented something better by now, but no… She sighed.

Once the pain settled into a repetitive throb, she released her hand, shaking it out for good measure. She looked down at the digit in question. The skin was red and abraded, already starting to swell. "That's gonna bruise." She fisted her hand, but the joint didn't want to bend.

Lacy smiled at her. "You hammered your finger again."

"It's really dark. I can barely see. Certainly not well enough to hit the bloody nails." She shook her head. "And it's frustrating. I finished most of this last night."

"You did?" Lacy's eyebrows rose, disappearing into her bangs.

Emma nodded. "Yeah. I stayed up late. Worked on completing a few buildings. I'd put the finishing exterior touches on six of the buildings before heading off to bed. But now? We had to rip them all down, throw all the damaged materials in a rubbish heap. Talk about a waste of effort. I went to bed yesterday feeling like we'd accomplished something and woke up defeated."

Lacy hugged her, patting her back and rocking her like a child. "I know, Emma. I know. We all feel that way. But it's only been one day. There'll be setbacks. We just have to overcome them."

Emma chuckled, shaking her head as Lacy mothered her, but she had to admit, her friend was right. "Yeah, I know." Her gut churned. "I just have this sinking suspicion we're setting ourselves up for a repeat performance."

Lacy leaned back, still holding Emma by the shoulders. "Well then maybe you should tell the captain."

Emma nodded. "I think I will." She shook out her hand once more and walked off in search of Captain West. She limped her way around the structure and the other workers, her foot still giving her trouble from dropping the metal siding on it yesterday. "Captain!"

West turned and sighed, shaking his head when he spotted Emma. "What is it now?"

Emma tried not to take offense. It wasn't anything personal. He was probably having a bad day, too. "I was just thinking we should set up a security patrol. To ensure this doesn't happen again."

"You think I wasn't already planning that?" He scoffed at her.

Bad move, Emma.

She shied backward. "Of course, sir. It wasn't my intention to question your ability to lead. I only meant to help."

He pointed his finger in her face. "You need to learn your place, pilot. *I* am the captain here. *I* am the leader. *Not* you."

Emma stiffened and ground her teeth, not wanting to undermine his authority, but there was a good reason she'd decided against joining the NSS. Sometimes, she just couldn't hold her tongue. It was a weakness. She knew it, but she just couldn't stop herself. "I *do* know my place, *Captain.* Maybe you should learn yours. You're responsible for the safety of every living person here. A *real* captain makes use of all their resources. Your behavior here today is unbecoming of an officer."

And on that note, she turned on her heel and stormed off.

West watched as his pilot stomped across the field, disturbing the people around her. Her boot heels hit the steps up to the ship with a clanging ring that echoed in the meadow. He sighed, unsure why she'd gone off on him… or why he'd gone off on her, for that matter.

He knew tensions were high. A lot of people were upset by this setback. He should have calmly told her he was already coordinating security patrols for tonight, not snap at her like that. She was right. That *wasn't* behavior becoming of an officer. If back on Earth, his superior would have chewed his ass out.

Rubbing his chin, he looked around. His heartbeat picked up in his chest. At first, all he noticed were people working, building their new home. Piles of metal filled the meadow, surrounded by blue and green vegetation that stood still and straight since there was no breeze today. Behind the piles, the skeleton of the new, single structure rose into the sky, its metal bones the carcass of yesterday's efforts.

Then other things came to him. Cursing. Yelling. Frustration and fear hung in the air. Most of them appeared calm enough with just pockets of negative emotion, but a deeper doom hovered over them like a black cloud heralding a storm. He could feel it, like smoke in the air, just enough to tickle one's throat. West shook it off, but it never quite left him.

Emma watched from the control room, trying to keep steam from streaming from her ears. Outside, people move around the meadow, business as usual. The contrast ramped her up even higher. She sat in the pilot's chair, listening to music on her headphones in a desperate attempt to calm down, but it didn't help.

Not that she'd chosen the ideal music for it. First, she'd started with dark music that was eerie, reminding her of Halloween and horror movies. Too on the nose for her frame of mind. Then she'd switched to something smooth and gentle, figuring it would put her at ease, but it just made her want to crawl out of her own skin. Finally, she settled on some hard rock music, yelling along with the lyrics. Screaming the words over and over again got it out of her system, though now her throat felt like sandpaper.

She listened to various artists sing about their obsessions with drugs and sex as everyone finished for the day, putting away tools and chatting as they migrated toward the ship. It didn't feel like they'd completed another day, though, time feeling distorted. She didn't notice when the sun set, but the sky had lost almost all of its color. Currently a deep purple, the expanse above was well on its way to midnight black. At least, she assumed so. They hadn't experienced true night on this planet yet. Who could say what it would be like?

Emma leaned forward, headphones still pressed into her ears, and looked up at the sky, looking for differences over the barely visible silhouettes of the treetops. Already, pinpricks of stars danced in the sky, and she contemplated laying down outside to soak up their ambiance, but didn't want to deal with people right now.

It could wait.

Dropping her gaze again, she spotted the captain outside, speaking to the security personnel and pointing at the trees. They nodded and saluted before dispersing, heading off in all directions. She caught one last glimpse of them as they disappeared into the woods and the captain entered the ship.

Seeing them dragged her mind from the night sky and to the destruction they'd found that morning. Her gut churned, fear snaking into her. Would they be all right? What if suggesting the patrol was a mistake? What if they were outgunned? Outmatched?

What if I get someone hurt? Killed?

Emma found it very difficult to sleep that night.

<hr>

He sighed, not looking forward to a full night spent on his feet, walking in circles. As a member of security, he knew this was part of the job, but he never liked it, never looked forward to it. He caressed the gun in his hand, feeling the cool, smooth metal as he patrolled the edge of the clearing.

Glancing over his shoulder at the new construction and the piles of irreparably damaged sheet metal, he wondered what he was up against. Was there some wild beast, a predator, lurking in the woods, waiting to strike? He stared into the trees, the deep darkness eerie and hypnotic. What was waiting for him there?

He lifted his gun higher, notching it to his shoulder, sighting along the top. He scanned the area for movement, but nothing disturbed the night other than the men on patrol. One of them was disappearing behind the corner of the building. Another was coming around the nose of the spaceship. Nothing else.

He frowned and continued his patrol, but his mind didn't turn off.

It shouldn't have happened.

He still couldn't believe it, waking up to all that damage. How? They'd put up a sensor grid. With something like that, anything larger than a rodent should have set it off, jerking him from sleep to run to the site's defense. But it had been quiet, unsettlingly so. How could they sleep through all that damage? Did the creature manage not to make a sound or had they been so dead tired they'd slept through it?

A horrible metal shriek sounded, and he froze, his gun pivoting toward the noise.

Go!

But it was already too late.

CHAPTER FIVE

DAY 3

*E*mma woke to someone standing over her bunk. "Gah!" She jumped, slamming her shoulder into a support beam. Well, at least it wasn't her head this time. She groaned, holding the joint where sharp pain screamed at her for seconds before dulling into background noise. She glared up at the intruder. "Was that really necessary?"

"Sorry. The crew wants to celebrate Christmas. I figure after the setbacks, we need it," Captain West said.

Emma's face fell. Bloody hell, what happened this time? "Have there been more setbacks?"

He nodded, then shook his head, his hands going to his hips in a superman pose. "I don't understand it. We had patrols the entire night. They didn't see a thing."

"They weren't hurt, were they?"

"No. No, they weren't hurt." He scoffed and turned away. As he spoke again, she didn't think he was actually talking to her, but mumbling under his breath, venting his own frustrations. "But we don't have enough supplies to keep on like this."

Emma stood, catching his attention. "Then we'll just have to get it from the surrounding areas. I mean, we've got lots of trees. We can use that, right?"

"You really have no idea how to just be a pilot." His smirk told her he wasn't cross for once.

"Nope. Sorry, Captain. I figure we all have to take on multiple roles out here."

"You're very wise. Just don't let it get you in trouble."

"Yes, sir!" She ended it with a mocking salute.

He shook his head. "Can you broadcast Christmas music over the intercom?"

She nodded. "That can be arranged."

"Excellent. See you in the mess hall."

"Yes, Captain."

West left, and Emma skipped over to the console. With a few clicks and the right code, "Silent Night" started broadcasting throughout the ship. With a great big smile on her face, she ran off to the mess hall, an extra pep in her step. "Morning, everyone," she said as she leaned into the room, letting the Christmas cheer surge through her like a child on Christmas morning.

The smell of spice and hearty foods permeated the air, triggering warm, fuzzy memories. She filled a plate and sat down, enjoying how people had come up with a wide variety of ways of making it festive. Someone had strung popcorn on string, while someone else had printed trees, stars, and reindeer and cut them out, sticking them to the walls and tables. Colored paper sat before bulbs to produce different colored light.

Children laughed and danced and ran. Lacy and her family hadn't arrived yet, so Emma sat alone. But the longer she sat, the more her expression fell and her mood died. A buffer zone surrounded her, an invisible barrier separating her from the rest of the people. Emma looked down at her food, torn between tears and rage.

Wanting to scream but refusing to make a scene, she stood and left the room. The first sniffle started when she entered the hallway. She started crying in earnest when she reached the control room, falling to the floor against the door.

What the hell is wrong with me?

She curled her arms around her knees, shaking her head at her own silliness. "I don't need them."

And yet the words couldn't stop the flood.

———

Emma composed herself and exited the ship to the captain barking out orders. His voice filled the meadow, clear as a bell. People in uniforms dashed off into the purple trees, axes and mauls in hand. She descended the stairs to stand next to West. "What can I do?"

"We're out of tools for cutting wood." He looked at her skeptically. Emma held her tongue, unwilling to comment on the sheer quantity of wood she'd cut and split in her lifetime. "Why don't you see what materials can be salvaged?"

"Yes, sir." She turned her back on the captain, looking to the building they were constructing, and lost hope. They'd lost all progress. Her hands flew to her mouth. "Oh my God," she whispered. How could so much damage be done in a single night? And without anyone the wiser?

The spotlights illuminating the field just made it seem worse, somehow. With intermittent light and shadow, it highlighted the damage, bringing it out in stark relief. Even the deep dark of night on this planet couldn't hide it.

After a moment, Emma shook off her shock and walked forward, a renewed determination in her step. Pushing up her sleeves, she started sorting through the loose pieces—putting them in piles based on usability and size once cut down.

By noon, her arms felt like butter, without the energy remaining to lift a bottle of water to her mouth or rub her tickling nose. "Oh, that is so annoying."

"What is it?" Lacy said as she dropped down beside her.

"I don't usually get allergies, but I think something here doesn't agree with me. I only started noticing it today."

"What is it?"

"Just… I feel like I have to sneeze. The feeling won't go away, though." She rubbed her nose again, that anticipatory feeling nagging at her, driving her mad.

Lacy shifted in place, leaning toward the *Endeavour*. "I've got some meds that might work."

Emma shook her head. "Nah. I don't like taking stuff."

Lacy laughed. "I never hear people say that."

Emma shrugged. "I'm not good at swallowing pills." Plus, it never seemed to work.

"Ah. I see."

"Thanks for the offer, though."

"What are friends for?"

Then a loud boom rang through the air, the concussion felt through the ground she sat on. Emma froze, dread filling her. "That wasn't a tree falling."

"It wasn't?" Lacy tensed beside her, bobbing her head back and forth as she searched for a cause.

"No." Emma stood and ran to the edge of the trees, hesitant to go any farther. "Hello? Is everyone all right? Is it safe to enter?" she yelled.

Nobody answered.

The echoes of the boom receded, though they still rang in her ears and memory. Her sense of duty overrode her sense of self-preservation, and she dashed into the trees, yelling, "Somebody answer me!" every few seconds.

Others followed her, dashing into the trees, but she didn't look behind her and soon their pounding steps dimmed. Trees whipped by, branches and leaves smacking against her arms as she jumped over roots, choosing her steps carefully as she navigated the uneven terrain. Everything was darkness, shadows, and the farther she traveled from the spotlights, the harder it became to see. Harder, but not impossible. Light didn't filter from above, but she could see silhouettes, outlines, and that was all she needed to keep going. She kept calling out, listening for a response, hoping for an answer.

After a few minutes, a disembodied voice yelled back, "No! Don't!"

Emma froze, nearly falling over as she stepped on a dime. Her side cramped from the running, and it took several minutes before her breathing calmed enough to speak. She glanced up and spotted an area of light off to the right. She'd been so focused on watching her feet that she'd missed it. "What happened?" Her heart pounded in her chest.

The voice was shaky, but close, male. "We're not sure. Maybe a landmine."

Emma stopped breathing, looking behind her at the distance she'd traveled unmolested. Bloody hell. She could have blown her legs off.

"He dropped the axe on the ground and it just blew, sending purple smoke into the air.

Purple smoke? That didn't sound right. What the hell type of explosive made purple smoke? For once, she really *felt* like the uneducated hotshot pilot. She'd never been big on science growing up and being homeschooled, living on a farm, it hadn't been that important.

"Okay. Is anyone hurt?" Maybe the explosion had been minor.

Please let it be minor.

She grabbed the bag around her waist, digging into it, but even the painkillers she always kept wouldn't come close to helping if the person was seriously injured. And the first aid supplies? Wouldn't do for much more than superficial burns.

"Yes."

Yes? What did that mean, "yes"? She'd lost her train of thought, lost track of the conversation. *Right, injuries. Someone was injured.* "How badly? Can you all walk? Do we need stretchers?" She looked back behind herself again. How far had she come? The trees looked more silhouetted in that direction, cast against a lighter gray background, but she couldn't see the lights from the meadow. If they couldn't walk, how would they get back? What if they encountered another explosive?

"Adam can't walk, but we can carry him back between us."

A little of the tension left her, but they still had the challenge of getting back. She felt like she was in a minefield without a map.

Because you are.

Hell.

"Okay. Walk as close to the location of the explosion as you can. That's the location least likely to have any explosive ordinance." Her voice trembled, giving away her nerves.

"Do you have experience with this sort of thing?" He sounded desperate, desperate to believe, but also like he was trying to delude himself.

She scoffed. "Not as much as I'd like."

He chuckled, the expression dry and humorless. "I bet."

She continued her instructions, speaking as the thoughts came to her. "Follow each other's footsteps. If you can remember places you've stepped before, choose those. They're probably safer."

Please, God, let us get out of this.

"Aye, aye, ma'am."

Emma took a deep breath, trying not to let them hear. She didn't want them to know how terrified she was. Looking at the ground with apprehension and suspicion, she took each step as if it would be her last.

The way back proved slow and interminable. The injured man moaned endlessly, putting everyone else on edge. Emma didn't look back, afraid of what she might see. The scent of burnt skin wafted to her, telling her what she would likely find. She'd seen plenty of gruesome things on her parents' farm, but seeing an injured animal was different than an injured human. It was too easy to imagine that injury being her own.

So instead of sight, she kept track of the others through sound —the gentle thud of footsteps, rasping breaths, the scrape of clothing against rough bark.

Good Lord! How far had they walked into the tree line? And why?

Emma's heart pounded in her chest, her limbs jerking into each new position. Whoever had called fear a superpower was clearly delusional. Right now, she'd be lucky not to fall on her face.

"We'll be there in no time," she lied for herself as much as for her companions. Purple bark and shaded ground stretched in all directions, eclipsing her view of the world. For all she knew, they weren't even going in the right direction. It was hard to see the lighter gray of the meadow, her eyes struggling with the bright light at her back.

A faint growl tickled at her eardrums, and she jumped, clutching a nearby tree. A high-pitched noise that definitely was not a squeal slipped from her lips.

Someone laughed behind her, the pain in the sound telling her who. "That was the girliest sound I've ever heard."

"Yeah?" She wanted to make a comeback, but one look silenced her. They had bigger problems, and a little laughter at her expense wouldn't hurt. But his comment only distracted her for a moment, and soon their problems poured back in on her like sand. She couldn't forget that something on this planet had destroyed all those building materials. Something strong enough to tear through sheet metal. Something that didn't want them here.

The tension started to make her shoulders cramp, and she had the strong urge to cry from the stress. But sometimes life didn't give you the luxury of breaking down. Even when you felt like you couldn't go on, time just kept moving forward, proving you wrong.

Then a group of men stormed up in front of them, and they all screamed, startled by the sudden appearance.

"Jesus, fuck. What the hell?" she said, holding her chest to keep her heart from fleeing.

"What happened?" the one at front said.

Getting her breathing under control, she looked them over. They were all members of the security team. She shook her head. "There was an explosion." She waved her hand behind them.

He nodded, moving to go past them.

"Wait!" She reached out a hand as if to stop him. "It's not safe. There was no obvious ordinance."

He tensed. "A minefield?"

"Maybe. I don't know. I'm just trying to get them back in one piece." *Mostly.*

He studied the others, taking in the injuries, and looked back at her. "Can you get back on your own?"

She nodded. "Yeah, I think we can." She might die of fright first, not knowing if her next step would be her last. But as long as nothing they stepped on went boom, they could make it.

He nodded and signaled the rest of his team. They moved like a wave around her group, disappearing quickly into the trees. Emma let out a sigh and continued forward again.

Moments dragged into minutes, and minutes multiplied into infinity. The coarse feel of bark under her fingertips steadied her, keeping her grounded when even the continuance of life seemed uncertain. The ground under her feet rose and fell from the growth of the trees' roots. Nothing else felt safe to walk on. The dirt could hold a thousand terrible things hell-bent on her destruction.

As adrenaline waned and logic regained its hold on her, she hugged the trees tighter. She figured it was less likely that ordinance would be hidden among the tree roots where people were unlikely to walk. She counted her breaths, measuring them to her steps to control the panic that threatened to bubble up every time she lost her focus. Moans and grunts continued behind her, telling her the injured man remained conscious, and digging at her conscience for not helping them carry him.

The roots and uneven terrain stabbed at her feet, her boots designed for navigating ships, not the outdoors. Her hands continued to brush coarsely over the bark beside her, using the trees almost to keep her upright.

She sighed a breath of relief when the lights from the *Endeavour* bled through the trees, like sunlight seeping through clouds after a storm. Growing up, she'd always thought it looked like God's fingers reaching down toward Earth. Now, it lightened her heart, making her dizzy with relief.

A few minutes later, they stumbled out of the trees. Emma barked out for aid, not really hearing her own voice, not really seeing anything as people laid the injured man on the grass. The tall grass hid his injuries from sight, then people rushed around him, hiding the rest of him.

She'd never felt more alone as she stood in the nearly waist-deep vegetation. A light breeze blew the blades across her legs, leaving little bits of fluff from seed pods on her clothes.

Emma looked to the trees again. What *had* that explosion been? What had caused it? Did some indigenous people set it as a trap? She turned back to the ravaged buildings with their claw marks, but swiveled her head back as she caught movement in her periphery. Squinting, she scoured the trees, but the light from the ship wouldn't let her see a nail, let alone reach into the depths of the thick grove.

CHAPTER SIX

DAY 4

*E*mma woke and chuckled to herself. This was the first time in days she hadn't hurt herself waking up. She rubbed the weariness from her face as best she could, but it ran bone deep, frustration and hopelessness taking their toll like a couple of maniacal twin boys.

Standing carefully from her bunk, she approached the Smart-Glass and peeked out, but the world outside had lost its luster. Where before she'd seen promise, hope, a new start, now she saw an endless series of calamities that just made her feel useless.

The horizon had lightened some, but no other evidence of the sun's turn graced the sky. It would rise today. She looked forward to working by daylight. Meandering through the ship, she passed no one. "They must already be up and working."

Upon reaching the mess hall, she grabbed some bread product and shoved it in her mouth, then snagged a bottle of water. The tasteless bread gummed up around her teeth. She gulped water to wash it down as she headed outside to help, hesitant to discover what added calamity would greet her this day. She paused at the door leading outside, munching on her bread more slowly as she racked her mind for what else could go wrong.

With a shrug, Emma gave up wondering and pushed through, breath bated as she walked down to greet Lacy. "What's the news?" She sat down on a beam and continued to eat, setting the bottle at her feet.

"Last night was quiet." Lacy seemed almost stunned at the news, as if waiting for the other shoe to drop.

"Well, we didn't exactly get a lot done yesterday."

"No, we didn't. I still can't believe you ran out into those trees. Weren't you afraid?"

Emma shrugged, not comfortable with this line of questioning. "I just reacted." She shoved another bite in her mouth, hoping Lacy would get the hint.

But of course, she didn't. Lacy sighed. "And that's what makes you so much better than me." She sounded morose and a little wistful.

Emma nearly choked on her food. "Wha—?"

Lacy nodded. "It's true. It was your first instinct to run out there, to run toward danger, all to help someone who's probably treated you like shit from the moment he met you." Lacy, sweet, sweet Lacy, snarled when she mentioned the person who'd been injured. It was adorable, like watching a Yorkie growl.

Emma blushed, but didn't deny it. God. Lacy made her sound like some kind of fucking hero. She coughed into her fist and changed the subject. "I feel like I got up late. What has everyone been doing?"

Lacy shrugged. "Some of the scientists entered the forest with security personnel, trying to figure out what caused the explosion. The captain won't let anyone leave the meadow until they've figured it out, and he feels it's safe. Which means we're left sitting here lollygagging because we've run out of material. And *that* seems to be messing with people." She frowned, her gaze straying out into the distance.

Emma looked around, her eyebrows rising at the escalating tension around her. People were snapping at each other. She half expected them to break out into fist fights at any moment. Many of them sat in a circle, chatting agitatedly about some monster.

A clap of sound made Emma start. She swiveled toward the source, thinking another explosion had gone off. A man rubbed his cheek in the distance while a woman stormed off in a huff toward the ship. She relaxed.

False alarm.

"Tensions really are high. I haven't seen them like this before." Emma had received a less than stellar reception from the party as a whole, but none had treated her that shoddily.

What the hell was going on?

The scientists and security personnel stepped out of the trees just as the sun cleared the mountains. "I wonder what they found." Emma wrung her hands, needing to move in the worst way. All the negative energy was winding her up.

Lacy grinned at her. "Maybe we should find out." She jumped to her feet and slinked off to where the scientists were joining Captain West.

Emma cursed under her breath and chased after her. "Lacy," she called out between gritted teeth.

Lacy just turned and smiled at her before sneaking closer.

"Nitrogen triiodide," one of the scientists said as Emma came close enough to hear.

"And what the hell is that?" the captain asked, crossing his arms over his chest.

But Emma knew. She would have never made the connection herself, but she remembered the word from a video she'd seen once. The scientist had placed a black powder out and then tapped it with a long stick, causing an explosion of purple smoke. "A touch explosive," she murmured. She didn't remember it being a terribly big explosion, though.

"That's correct," the scientist said, a look of blatant surprise crossing his face at the lowly pilot knowing that.

Heat suffused her cheeks, not having realized she'd spoken loud enough to be heard, but she decided to go on anyway, seeing as stealth was no longer an option. "It's highly unstable and can be stabilized by…" She paused, trying to remember the chemical from the video. "What was it? It's nitrogen-based, I remember that."

The scientist nodded. "That's right. Ammonia." He turned to the captain. "I suggest we step nowhere in the forest where the ground is dry."

"Only step where you can smell piss," Emma chimed in.

A chagrined look crossed the scientist's face, but he nodded once more, his shoulders sagging at her wording, she supposed.

"Piss?" the captain asked.

She shrugged. "Well, old piss."

The captain shook his head. "How are we going to harvest materials? If we fell a tree in those woods, it could cause an explosion."

Emma chewed her lip, just as puzzled, but then an idea struck her. "We've trampled all over this meadow. There can't possibly be any here. We would have blown ourselves to kingdom come by now."

"And?" The captain glared at her, impatience tensing his muscles.

"We just control the drop, make sure it drops toward the meadow. Anyone who's ever cut down a tree knows how." At least anyone with a lick of sense. It would be right foolish and dangerous to drop a tree without knowing it wouldn't fall on your house.

"And how are we supposed to manage that?"

Emma's jaw dropped. He didn't know? Surely, the people he'd sent out to cut down trees knew that, right? He should have at least known it was *possible*. "Well, first you tie off the tree high up and stake it so it can't fall in the wrong direction. Then you chop it so it's weakest on the side you want it to fall on."

"Can you show the others how?"

Emma's eyes went wide. Had the captain been abducted by aliens or something? She just couldn't fathom him asking for *her* expertise. Up til now, the only assistance he'd requested was controlling parts of the ship. She nodded, a little dazed.

"Good. That's settled. The pilot will train people on felling the trees toward the meadow. Let's get to it."

Emma bristled at being called pilot again. He'd finally seen the merit of her other skills, but he still couldn't be bothered to remember her name?

The rising sun made work easier and easier, casting brilliant hues across the sky. As if by contrast, the men became increasingly irritable, cursing and snarling at each other like a pack of wolves. Twice now, she'd had to break up fights, though how she'd managed it, she had no clue.

Emma wasn't small, but all the men chosen to help fell trees towered over her, outstripping her in both height and muscle. It would only take a single blow to knock her senseless.

"That's it," a man yelled to her right.

She bristled, knowing another fight was about to break out. Turning, she dashed forward, trying to separate the two men. But their reach far exceeded her own, and they landed blows even with her arms outstretched, pressed to each man's chest. Sweaty fabric pressed against her palms, making her hands slip as she tried fruitlessly to keep them apart.

"What the fuck?" one of them said, aiming for his attacker, but hitting her instead.

The breath flew from her, and she couldn't even register where she'd been hit. She panicked as she collapsed to the ground, narrowly avoiding being trampled as more men joined in over her head. Her oxygen-starved brain screamed at her to move as a dog pile like in a cartoon formed above her. Crab walking between swinging limbs and stomping feet, she prayed she would be like the intended victim in those toons. They always seemed to slip out from beneath their attackers as the fighters continued to pummel each other in a cloud of fists, feet, and dust.

But this was reality, not a cartoon, and she didn't know what to do as she finally got her breath back and stood. Her heart still pounded in her chest, making her entire body shake with adrenaline. People rushed to the scene, but instead of trying to break up the fight, they cheered them on, leaving Emma slack-jawed in shock. She couldn't believe her eyes. What was wrong with these people? Had they gone mad?

They must have, she concluded as more men joined the fray. Not knowing what else to do, she turned and jogged away, hoping for an authority figure who might set the situation to rights. She spotted the captain racing forward and yelled, "Do something!" her voice still breathy from the blow she'd taken.

It all felt surreal, like a dream she very desperately wished she could wake from. Covering her ears, unable or unwilling to hear the continued cheers accompanying the sounds of violence, she walked shakily away. Her gait increased to a jog as she approached the ship with ever increasing urgency.

Lacy sighed in relief when she found Emma in the control room, sitting on the bottom bunk and staring at a wall. "Are you all right?" she said, her voice breathy with concern. She could still see the bloody mess in her mind's eye after they finally broke up the fight outside. Bloody lips, swollen eyes, bruising everywhere. The sharp, coppery tang of their injuries overshadowed the sweet smell of the meadow. She'd been shocked stupid.

Then she'd discovered the group that started it had been learning to take down trees from Emma, her friend. Emma had *been* there. Terrified her friend was hurt as well, she'd searched the crowd, only to find no signs of her. After a lot of questioning, mostly with people who barely grunted in response, she'd learned the captain had seen Emma moving toward the ship.

"What has gotten into everyone?" Emma said, throwing her hands up in the air.

Lacy shook her head and sat near her friend, the thin mattress shifting under her butt. "I don't know. Maybe it's just frustration or fear. Those can do terrifying things to people." But even that didn't seem like a good enough explanation. Even after the incident, after everyone seemingly calmed down, there was still a frenetic energy about the group. It felt like all it would take was a questionable look and another fight would break out. It didn't make any sense.

Emma only nodded in response, making Lacy sigh. She wanted to cheer her friend up, but doubted she could. Things had spiraled further and further off course ever since they'd landed on this Godforsaken rock. So, instead, she reached out and urged Emma to rest her head on Lacy's shoulder, making soft, soothing sounds as she rocked her.

Things would turn around.

They had to.

Lacy managed to drag Emma out of the control room in time for supper. They'd spent a good deal of time sitting on that bed while her frayed nerves tried to knit themselves back together again. It had taken time, but Emma had appreciated the comfort, the feel of another being's warmth, the pressure of a hug, as she pulled herself together. She squeezed her friend's arm, smiling at her as a thank you.

"I'm glad you can smile again."

Emma laughed and shook her head. "Sorry about that. It was just… too much." She could still feel echoes of the panic that consumed her as she dropped to the ground, large bodies looming over her as she scrambled to escape. She shivered remembering it.

"Trust me, Emma. I understand." Lacy wagged her finger at her. "I'm married, and I have a little girl. Sometimes, I just want to wash my hands of the two." She chuckled affectionately.

Emma shook her head. "This was different, though." Her mind drifted back to that moment before the first strike hit. "It was like there was this manic energy in the air. I've never felt anything like it."

Lacy frowned. "I know. It was weird. And someone died."

"What?" Emma turned, grasping her friend by the shoulders. "Someone died?"

She nodded. "One of the men fighting. By the time they broke up the fight, he wasn't moving."

Ice ran through Emma's gut, and she had the slightest urge to throw up, but she resisted. "Who?"

"I didn't know him, but I gather he was recruited to cut down trees."

Her mind's eye drifted to the man who'd said, "What the fuck?" Was it him? But then, what did it matter? She didn't know any of them, not really. "I'm starting to wish we'd never come here."

"Now, Emma. It's not that bad."

"Not that bad? Are you kidding? A man has died."

Lacy nodded. "And another may never walk again."

"What?"

"I overheard it earlier today. The man who stepped on the… chemical. They think he might never walk again, especially this far from advanced medical treatment."

"Nitrogen triiodide," Emma said absently. She shook her head. "We made a terrible decision in coming here."

"Oh, Emma. Every expedition has its problems."

She gave her friend the stink eye. "This is more than just problems, Lacy. One man is dead, another may never walk again, and almost all our materials have been shredded by some mysterious beast who only comes out when we're fast asleep." Which was especially troubling because it didn't match the circadian rhythms of this planet. Wouldn't an animal follow the patterns of the day cycle?

"Well, yes, but…"

"No but. There's something very wrong here. We're not prepared for this planet. It's going to get us killed. All of us."

Lacy sighed. "Well, yeah, with that type of attitude."

Emma scoffed. "I'm just a realist, Lacy. I can be as optimistic as the next person, but reality is never far from mind."

Lacy sighed again, but seemed to let it go, leading Emma outside, where people were eating. Her gaze drifted to the area near the trees where the fight had broke out. The grasses were trampled flat and, in some spots, the vegetation had been ripped out in patches, speaking to the struggle that occurred there earlier that day.

Emma held her tongue, but her mind kept screaming they never should have come here. People had died, and she had a sinking feeling that if something didn't change, more deaths were on the horizon.

CHAPTER SEVEN

DAY 5

*E*mma woke to screams again, causing her to jerk up in bed and slam her head. "Mother fucker!" she said, clutching her forehead as she rolled off the mattress with an umph. Letting the pain ebb, she started to register voices crying out in panic outside. Tenderly testing her forehead, her fingers came away coated in a splotch of blood.

She groaned, but crawled to her feet and peeked outside through the SmartGlass. "Bloody hell!" She raced out of the control room, the red glow in the field still forefront in her mind.

Fire! The field was on fire.

When she reached the stairs leading down to the meadow, she paused, not knowing what to do. She'd never been confronted with a situation like this before. They hadn't even searched out natural resources yet, other than chopping trees. From her descent to the planet the first day, she knew bodies of water sat nearby, but with all the setbacks, no one had looked for them.

Which just left the resources on the *Endeavour*. She turned and reached for the console next to the door. With flying fingers, she plowed through the controls until she managed to access the fire suppression system. It was intended to douse fires inside the ship, but also had some small controls for dousing fires outside in case an engine caught fire in atmosphere. Unfortunately, the external systems were very precise, and would need tweaking and repurposing to put out fires in the field.

If they could…

She didn't know if it was possible. Did they have the force, the reach? Could she get an appropriate angle? Could she cover the entire field?

After a few minutes, she'd changed the system settings, increasing the pressure and spray duration, and allowing for non-automated and separate control of each component. Emma dashed out the door toward the nozzle near the left thruster, the only one close to the fire. She yanked it out of its housing, wincing as it groaned and thin pieces of metal snapped under her hands. With a little bit of tape from the bag she kept on her waist at all times, she forced it into position and ran back to the control panel.

Emma slammed her hand against the panel and jumped out the door again. She breathed a sigh of relief when fire suppressant foam jetted from the nozzle, arcing across the distance, coating plants and people alike. In moments, the fire died. She waited a few more to make sure it stayed dead, then returned to the panel to turn off the nozzle, letting out a sigh of relief.

She was glad the fire was out, but didn't look forward to fixing the fire suppression system later…

Emma was sitting on the steps as Lacy sat down to join her. It was still morning, and she had just collapsed after inspecting the nozzle housing she'd damaged. In the heat of the moment, she'd thought nothing of the metal strips snapping off when she'd yanked the nozzle out. Now, she couldn't figure out how she'd done it. The metal was strong and heat resistant despite its thin nature. She couldn't imagine *how* she'd broken it. She rolled one of the sharp bits of metal in her hand, rubbing her fingers over the smooth surface.

Maybe it's like those stories of people lifting cars to rescue children.

She shrugged, pushing it out of her mind. Emma had more pressing things to worry about… like how to repair the housing. Because it was so heat resistant, she wasn't sure she had the tools to repair it. The metal required special welding tools. She doubted they had them on board.

"That was quick thinking, Emma. Thank you."

Emma jerked her head up to meet her friend's gaze, having forgot Lacy had sat down next to her, and waved away the appreciation. She wished she could have woken faster, or that she hadn't stood there dumbfounded at the door taking it all in. Could she have mitigated some of the damage?

She lifted her gaze to the meadow. The acrid smell of smoke overwhelmed the normally sweet smell she'd grown accustomed to. Where before blue and green grasses had stood as tall as one's hips, now most of the plants were burned to the ground. A haze drifted in the air, probably smoke and remnants of burnt plants. Several of the buildings had gaping holes where they had supplemented supplies with local trees.

Lacy sighed. "People aren't taking it well."

Emma scoffed. "How could they? Practically every day they find more of their efforts destroyed. Even the greatest optimist would be downtrodden by now." And Emma wasn't exactly an optimist.

"That's true." She shook her head. "They keep sniping at each other, though, and going on and on about 'The Beast.' About how it'll get them in their sleep."

"Oh?" Emma turned to Lacy. She remembered some people talking about a monster recently. Was that the same thing?

Emma looked out to the trees as she forced her thoughts away from the so called beast, a little anxiety growing in her chest, but she didn't let her friend know. She rolled her eyes, thinking back to what Lacy had just said about being attacked in their sleep, and snorted. "Yeah, that's bloody likely."

Lacy laughed. "That's pretty much what I said. Which is when I got my head bitten off and decided to wait for you."

"Well, never fear. If I bit your head off, rest assured, there would be PMS involved."

Lacy laughed, clutching her stomach as she rolled back and forth in her seat.

Emma smiled and shook her head, but the mirth was marred by the tense atmosphere around them.

———

Work dragged on after the fire, fraying people's nerves as they grew increasingly exhausted. Smoke made it difficult to breathe, and unfortunately, they had no breeze to clear the air. By the evening meal, anxieties had reached a peak.

For once, they didn't linger in the field to eat, preferring the mess hall. Emma followed, but felt uneasy. She grabbed a tray of food, not even registering its contents, and sat at a small table in the corner, her back to the wall. The holiday decorations had long since been taken down, leaving bare, utilitarian walls with only their clothing to give sparks of color. The room quickly filled with bodies and the echoing cacophony of many voices talking at once.

People all around her whispered of "The Beast." They'd made good progress that day, and everyone feared him striking again. While she, too, felt a certain level of depression at their efforts being thwarted once again, she was puzzled at their reactions.

The fear seemed amplified, like some demon was poking at their psyches with a stick, their feelings having morphed until they resembled a frenzied mob. And their focus wasn't even on their efforts being destroyed as the meal waxed on. Instead, they seemed positive that "The Beast" would attack them in their sleep. Shock left her jaw slack, and she kept forgetting to chew. What had gotten into them? Lacy had mentioned the same thing earlier, but it had sounded so ludicrous, so insane. An overwhelming urge to run rushed through her.

"I've got a bad feeling about this," Lacy said as she sat down next to Emma, parroting her innermost thoughts.

"So do I, Lacy. So do I."

CHAPTER EIGHT

DAY 6

$\mathcal{B}$eeyun stood watch outside the alien camp, feeling dejected. Even after multiple attempts, the foreigners showed no signs of leaving. When he'd arrived earlier, he'd intended to do his regular bout of damage, but he'd hesitated, shocked at the state of the field. The maenu was blackened, burnt to the ground. He wanted to drive them all away for the damage they'd already done, but hesitated. He covered his mouth as he stood watch, not wanting to breathe in the nasty maenu spores that were released in droves by the fire. Looking at the field afterward, it didn't seem necessary to add more destruction. What could he do that was worse than they'd already done to themselves?

But what had caused it?

He stared out over the field, searching for likely sources of ignition. There had been no storm earlier, thus no lightning. And while he wanted to rid himself of these beings, he would have never lit fire to the field. Maenu was a nasty plant under the best of circumstances, but it triggered a defense mechanism under stress, as it would during a fire. He watched as the foreigners became increasingly agitated, a likely direct result of the poisonous exposure.

He couldn't get close, though. Not until the maenu calmed down a bit. It wasn't safe.

And yet some did not succumb. Mostly, he noticed that the brave one, the one that ran *toward* the pyor explosion, she did not succumb. In fact, she seemed confused by the actions of her compatriots, to the point of losing patience with them. She crossed the burnt black field, looking listless as the others moved erratically around tasks he could not fathom. The fire had burned holes in their buildings, but the shiny beast seemed in pristine condition, other than some black smudges. She seemed listless, and he wanted to reach out and soothe her.

He frowned, but kept quiet and still in place, knowing the foreigners deserved whatever punishment the maenu dealt out, even his brave one.

By the end of the day, Emma was skittish as all get out, her muscles trembling with the tension permeating the air. People yelled at each other, threw punches, and through it all, they seemed to blame every offense on "The Beast." Whisperings surrounded her, and a tightness built in her chest.

She walked across the field to Lacy and grabbed her by the arm, lifting her to her feet. "Take your family and get inside. Lock yourselves somewhere no one can get to you."

"Emma? What's wrong?" Her friend stood slowly, too slowly.

Emma shook her head and looked around again, but nothing had changed. What was wrong with everyone? "I don't know.

I've just got this really bad feeling, like all hell is about to break loose."

Lacy nodded. "I know what you mean. Things have been rough all day." Lacy's gaze shifted to the distance and her face fell. She grabbed onto Emma's arm, her voice hesitant, scared. "Emma? Emma, they're all looking over here."

She froze, afraid to turn around. "What do you mean?" What did they want?

"I don't know, but it doesn't look good." Lacy's voice was barely above a whisper.

Emma wanted to turn but lacked the courage to look. On some level, she knew, but she also didn't want to accept it. "Go inside, Lacy." Her voice was like steel as she spoke. She didn't want her friend to see them turn on her, and scenes from <u>The Lord of the Flies</u> kept popping into her head. People tended to turn on the outcast when times got tough.

"Go."

Lacy moved to collect her family, but it was already too late. She froze mid-motion, her eyes widening in horror.

Emma turned around, only to be hit with a hard fist across the face, nearly knocking her off her feet. Pain bloomed through her cheek, then stabbed through her scalp as another hand grabbed at her hair, yanking at it ruthlessly. Emma couldn't quite make out the vicious voices around her, or what they said. Another blow landed, knocking her to the ground. She was now being dragged by her hair. Her scalp screamed at her, and she tried grabbing at the hand holding her but it was no use.

Lacy screamed, but it only formed yet another backdrop on the scene.

The person let go of her hair, and Emma let out a breath of relief, clutching her head to ease the throbbing, but the relief was short-lived. Arms grabbed her, tying her up until the wire tore into her wrists and ankles. She tried to break free, but it only made the wire dig deeper.

Finally free of their hands, she looked around her. For a moment, a calm overcame her, and she didn't fear. The relief from no longer being manhandled left her lightheaded and slow to pick up on the minutiae of her predicament. People yelled, hatred turning their faces red and purple. She'd never seen so much animosity in one place. How could any one person contain such rage? What was happening to them?

But gradually little details, words plucked from the air, flashed into her brain, lighting off understanding and dawning horror.

Sacrifice.

Beast.

Outsider.

Die.

Fear leaped up in her chest once more, and she turned to her friend, who was fighting to reach her, fighting to help her. A sea of people stood between the two of them, keeping them apart. The sea writhed with anger and motion, just as chaotic as the sound of their unified voices. She stared at Lacy, her friend. Emotion welled, and Emma shook her head. She didn't want her friend to get hurt, too. She didn't want Jacie to witness this, or worse, see Lacy suffer the same fate. Emma took a deep breath, steadying herself, resigning herself to her fate. "Go," she mouthed.

Lacy stopped, her lower lip trembling. She shook her head, her shaky hand rising to her mouth in a defensive move. "No," she mouthed back.

But Emma just repeated herself. "Go."

She couldn't save herself, but she could save her friend, she could save that cute little girl.

Lacy broke into a sob and backed away as tears poured down her cheeks. She finally turned, grabbed her family, and ran for the ship.

Emma closed her eyes and took a deep breath, not willing to let these people see her weakness. If she was going to die at their hands, she would be strong. She would not give them the pleasure of knowing her fear.

CHAPTER NINE

Beeyun watched the brave woman who'd run toward the pyor explosion. Hardworking and brave, he couldn't help but admire her. He could admire an enemy, couldn't he? He also felt guilty, though, knowing she was foreign and just as bad as the rest. She would destroy his world just the same as her friends would. He knew that.

And yet he couldn't stop watching over her. She'd looked like a goddess as she streaked through the trees, her cheeks flushed an odd red color he found appealing, her hair flowing back behind her. She'd traversed the terrain as if she were born to it, and he regretted that they couldn't talk. He had no way to convince her she should abandon whatever fool mission she'd undertaken.

Now, to see her trussed up as a raging mob surrounded her, anger tinged his cheeks almost black. Beeyun had vowed to stop them. He'd even felt the maenu's wrath was righteous punishment for their actions, but in his heart, he knew this brave one did nothing to earn *this* fate. He firmly believed she deserved better, and if one such as her received such an end, what hope did *he* have?

He'd stood there in the fringes as they grabbed her, hit her, then dragged her through the burnt maenu and debris to the last remaining structure. His muscles tensed each time, forcing himself to stand still. It took two men bigger than her to tie her to an upright support. The crowd formed in a semicircle around her, screaming their insanity to the winds.

He tensed and forced himself to crouch low, trying to decide what to do even though his body had long ago decided for him. What could he do? His extended claws dug into the soft dirt, telegraphing his tension. She was a foreigner, just as guilty as the rest.

He kept telling himself that. Why did he feel the need to keep reiterating it?

Because I don't really believe it…

He couldn't believe it, not with her trussed up like that. She was a victim. She didn't deserve this. No one deserved this.

In the blink of an eye, his decision was made, though he couldn't say what ultimately moved him. Was it her bravery? Her hard work? Her grace?

Or did he think he could learn from her, get her to see reason? Did he think he could get them to stop through her?

In a burst of speed, he dashed across the field, heading straight for the brave one. He unleashed his claws and swung his arm as he approached, slicing through metal as if it were butter. The pieces fell to the ground, releasing her, and he scooped her up, continuing on to the trees on the other side.

Lacy ran into the control room with her family, locking the door behind her. It was the only room she knew she could lock and keep locked. She silently thanked God Emma had given her the door codes a while back, saying Lacy would always have a quiet place if she needed it. Emma had joked that, with her family, she would probably need it eventually. Lacy couldn't even find the humor in the memory anymore. She swiped at her wet cheeks and raced to the SmartGlass. "I'm such a coward."

"No, you're not," her wife said, resting a hand on her shoulder.

Outside, the nightmare continued. She wanted to turn away. She didn't want to see her friend hurt anymore. "I should be protecting her, helping her." Someone needed to go out there, to stop them. What was wrong with everyone?

Rickelle dropped her hands on Lacy's shoulders from behind, digging her fingers in reassuringly. "You're doing what she wanted you to do—protecting your family."

Lacy nodded, trying to internalize Rick's words, but it was hard. It felt wrong to run, to leave Emma behind. Tears welled in her eyes again, blurring the hellish scene before her. *Good.* She didn't want to watch. But as she looked out, a dark streak flew across the meadow, taking Emma with it. She screamed. "No!"

"What? What is it?" her wife, holding her, leaned over her shoulder to see, her body pressed into Lacy's back.

Jacie cried in the background, but they were momentarily too engrossed in the drama to soothe her.

"She's gone." Lacy's voice cracked. "Something took her."

Beeyun ran through the thick forest with ease. He tried shifting his burden to a more comfortable position, but her tied hands and feet made it almost impossible, so he simply held her close and headed for home.

As he ran, her warmth seeped into him, and he found it so strange that she was neither screaming her head off nor struggling. Perhaps she realized he'd saved her and was grateful. Or perhaps she was waiting for the opportune moment to escape. After all, until the restraints were removed, she would have little luck in fighting or escaping.

His long strides devoured the distance, and he found himself marveling at how very small she was. Spying on them as he had the last two days, he hadn't realized how tiny their species was. She'd seemed fairly tall compared to the rest of her people, but she felt like a child in his arms—small, fragile.

It felt wrong, so at odds with his perception of her in his mind. She was his brave one. Proud, strong, graceful. She was everything he wasn't. It was a hard fact to admit, even in his own head.

They reached his home, which looked like a hole in the side of a mountain from the outside, and he slowed, carefully entering so as not to hurt her accidentally. He walked through to the kitchen and set her down. Reaching for her hands, he sliced through the metal binding them with the claws he still had extended. He crouched down and repeated the act with her ankles. Bits of metal dropped to coil against the smooth, stone floor at her feet.

When he stood to his full height, she was looking up at him with curiosity and awe as she rubbed absently at her wrists. Beeyun felt uncomfortable. He didn't deserve awe. He'd expected her to be terrified or fight him now that she was free, so he stood dumbfounded at her expression. When she reached out to touch him, he didn't even think, he just bent down so she could reach his face.

Beeyun's gaze never left her face as she ran gentle, questing fingers across his features. In that moment, he knew he would do whatever he could to help her, to care for her. He would keep her safe. Her compatriots would never find her here, couldn't hurt her here, and he had sufficient food for them both. She would never want for anything.

He shuddered, the image of her tied up in the middle of that mob popping into his head again. What were they going to do to her? Would they have left her out to starve or die of dehydration? Would they have beaten her to death? A chill ran along his skin at the idea, and he peered down at her once more. She was so brave. She'd stared them down without fear, even though she must have known how grim her fate was. He couldn't bear the idea that this brave female might have died today. There was something about her, something special. What type of world did he live in if something that special could be snuffed out like that?

Then his gaze caught on the abused wrist right next to his face. Beeyun touched her hand, drawing it down so he could see better. Whatever they'd tied her up with had dug into the skin, damaging her. He needed to clean the wounds, make sure they didn't get infected.

Alarm surged through him. How could he possibly keep such a fragile creature safe? He imagined all it would take was the first disease she contracted on this planet, and she would never recover. Even this tiny wound could get infected and prove deadly. His people were robust, far more robust than this tiny little thing, and yet even they sometimes were laid low by the illnesses here.

He shoved his emotions aside, focusing on the task at hand. First, he needed to treat her wounds. Then he could deal with her susceptibility to disease. He pressed his hands against her shoulders, trying to impress on her that he wanted her to remain here. When he stepped back, she stayed put, watching him as if ensnared. What did she see when she looked at him? There was no fear like he would expect of an alien. But there was also an appreciation he'd never experienced, even among his own people. "Brave one, stay, please."

She gave him a hesitant smile as he grabbed a bowl from the cupboards and headed to the bathroom for supplies. He rushed around, grabbing what he needed, tripping over his own limbs in his rush to get back to her, afraid she would be gone. When he dashed back into the kitchen, he let out a breath of relief when she was still standing where he'd left her, an odd expression on her face.

Beeyun dropped to his knees in front of her, resting his supplies on the floor. With careful concern, he washed her wrists and ankles. She cringed, but kept quiet, letting him work in peace. Before long, he'd applied an antimicrobial cream and layered it with soft bandages. He stood, continuing to run his fingers soothingly over her soft hands.

He was hesitant now, unsure what to do. He'd cared for her wounds, but that wasn't the only danger here on Ara. If she was susceptible to any of the native diseases, he couldn't imagine her surviving them. He, like most of his people, was immune to many of those maladies. Their species was well adapted, having a natural ability to share that resistance. Unfortunately, that was a very intimate act, one he couldn't imagine doing with someone he couldn't even talk to. And would she thank him or curse him afterward?

Probably curse him. She wouldn't understand, *couldn't* possibly understand. Beeyun looked down at her again, her hand still clasped between his. The smile on her face had grown. She looked up at him like he'd raised the mountains from the sea.

She won't reject me.

He reached down with one of his hands and caressed her cheek. *So soft.* She closed her eyes for only a moment, leaning into the touch. A long, deep breath puffed against his palm. She opened her eyes, staring at him again. Reaching up with the hand he wasn't holding, she touched the hand on her cheek, holding it there.

She wouldn't reject him, would she? She wouldn't understand why, but she wouldn't say no, right?

Think of it like a medical procedure. You're just doing it to keep her healthy.

Except, no matter how he tried to convince himself, he just couldn't see it as merely a medical procedure. Taking in those big eyes, those intriguingly tinted, soft lips, he didn't feel the least bit professionally detached. He *wanted* to do this. With a strange alien with very pale, brown skin.

What was wrong with him?

Beeyun leaned down, his breath fanning over her face, her lips. He could feel her hot, humid breath brush against his own skin in kind. She didn't pull away, and so he kissed her.

Her lips proved just as soft as they'd looked, and she moaned into his mouth. He reached around her and lifted her into his arms, caressing her as she responded in earnest to his ministrations.

No.

He shook himself, taking in her dazed expression. Her eyes looked different, brighter somehow. Eager?

It didn't matter. Without the ability to talk to her, without even knowing if she understood, he would just feel like a rapist. It didn't sit well with him. He let her slip down, settling on her feet, and took up her hand once more. He moved blindly to his bedroom, trying not to remember what she'd looked like in her ardor.

Once in the room, he didn't look as he pulled back the sheets and tucked her in, running a hand over her silky hair, moving it out of her face. She stared up at him, looking a little confused.

This was the right decision. She'd had a hard day, an exhausting one. More than anything else, she needed rest.

At least that he *could* provide.

———

Emma sat up in bed, a bit dazed from recent events. She'd been attacked by her own people, rescued by an alien, *kissed* by an alien, and left alone in someone else's bed. She felt like she'd been tossed to the winds.

Her hands curled in the sheets, grounding herself. She ran her fingers along surprisingly soft material.

He kissed me.

She couldn't quite escape that thought. It kept ringing through her head, keeping her constantly off balance.

And she'd liked it, too. She'd been attracted to him, fascinated by the contrasts in skin tone, his purple to her tan. And his skin had been soft, making her not want to stop. She'd never felt like that before, and she kind of wanted to explore it some more.

Emma stared at the empty doorway, wondering where he'd gone. He'd plopped her in bed, tucked her in, and disappeared. Unfortunately, she was too wired and unsettled to sleep.

She wanted to get up, explore, but hesitated. He'd put her in here for a reason. She didn't know if she would be welcome elsewhere, or how he would react if she disobeyed. He was an alien, after all. How could she possibly suss out his motivations?

So, instead, she let her gaze wander the room. It was… nice. The intricately carved wooden bed held a sturdy mattress that reminded her a bit of human technology. Beside it rested chests of drawers, equally beautiful and matching the bed. Lights lined the walls in a style similar to long, fluorescent tubes. Someone had carved the stone walls, inlaying jewels as decoration, giving it an earthy, yet luxurious appearance.

It did not speak to a backwater, primitive existence. It spoke of technology almost equal to their own. Possibly more advanced in some areas as they'd pulled this off without detracting from the natural beauty of their world. Guilt curdled in her stomach as she thought of the arrogance of humanity.

She thought of the alien the others had called "The Beast." Emma stood tall for a human female at 5'8", but this man had towered over her, probably at least seven feet tall. And while he had muscles rippling over his form, it was the physique of a runner. She smiled, remembering how he'd dashed across the field, rescued her, and then ran straight to his home without breaking stride.

Her heart had jumped in her chest when she saw him coming at her, assuming for a moment she was about to die. But he'd saved her, and though the ride here had been jarring, it had also given her time to think. And she realized he'd simply been trying to make them leave. They had stolen onto his property and tried to set up shop, and he just didn't want to let them.

Emma blushed as she realized again how presumptuous they'd
been.

"Why?" she asked no one in particular. "Why did you save
me?" It didn't make sense.

Why me?

CHAPTER TEN

*B*eeyun woke the next morning feeling exhausted, too exhausted to open his eyes. With the need to watch (and intervene with) the foreigners in the maenu meadow, he hadn't managed a full night's sleep in a couple days now. He'd gone to bed late the night before. It had been so late, he'd briefly wondered if it was even worth sleeping, but he couldn't go much longer without rest.

She'd been curled up, dead to the world, fascinating in her repose.

How could another species be so similar and yet so different? He'd never been much interested in science in school, but now he couldn't help wonder what made them so alike. What mechanics were at play? Would they be similar in other ways? What other ways were they different?

His eyelids were heavy as he finally opened his eyes. She was staring at him with this curious look on her face. He couldn't help feeling happy, grateful. "My brave one."

Her eyebrows arched at that, and he smiled. What was she thinking? He wished they could understand each other, but those things took time. She lay partially on top of him, but she made no move to create distance, an almost defiant look crossing her face. Beeyun reached out, held her face between his hands, and kissed her forehead. "I will keep you safe, my brave one." He shifted to the side, letting her slide off him. He really didn't want to leave. Her heat had melted into his bones, tempting him to stay entwined in bed forever, but that wouldn't be productive. Maybe he could help her learn to care for herself, teach her about his home. Or learn her language so he could speak with her. He could learn her name, what made her tick.

Instead, he sighed. He'd had enough setbacks lately. He couldn't forget they weren't the only ones on this planet. So far, he'd been unsuccessful in driving her people away as it was his duty to do.

Suddenly, his heart sank. He stood and dressed, his thoughts shifting reluctantly to the tasks ahead. He would see her taken care of and fed, then he needed to check on her people. There may be efforts he needed to thwart, and besides, his implant needed more exposure to her language before he could communicate with her. He suspected he would further the process more listening to an entire crowd than a single person.

Turning back to the bed, he motioned for her to get up, then left the room in search of a meal in the kitchen. As he pulled out fruit and bread, he wished he could protect her better, but while he could save her from physical harm, there was only one way to keep her healthy. His people simply didn't *need* another way. After all, if antibodies could be passed from person to person using bodily fluids, why would anyone invent another method? Mothers passed antibodies using breast milk and lovers via sex. A simple kiss could help, but the number and variety of antibodies was never as much in saliva as other fluids.

Should I have…

He couldn't even finish the thought. The kiss would have to be enough. His thoughts and emotions were tangled, though, leaving him struggling to find the right approach. He couldn't imagine having sex with someone he'd never spoken to. Living as he did, he didn't have many visitors, didn't see many people other than his brother. Still, he'd never had sex with someone he'd never had a conversation with before.

He wasn't about to start now.

Emma felt like she hadn't slept a wink. At one point, she'd found herself in bed with him, her savior, and she never went back to sleep. He was out cold, and she'd just watched him for hours, not sure what to do, but a plan had started forming in her head. Then one moment, she was marveling at his face, wondering about everything from his personality and culture to his anatomical differences, and the next, he was slipping off the bed and getting dressed.

Her mind was still reeling at his sudden wakefulness when he started talking to her in a language she couldn't understand. Then she realized he was dressed and gone.

Did he kiss my forehead?

While brief, the short "exchange" had been somewhat intimate. She could have imagined a couple waking up, the man kissing his partner's forehead and telling her not to get up as he got ready for work. It felt so… normal.

Emma blinked at the space he'd occupied only moments ago. She pushed the sheets aside, rubbing absently at the bandages on her wrists where the skin was still raw from the wire cutting in yesterday. She peeled the bandages away. Like usual, the cuts were little more than angry red spots now, but they still smarted.

Moving on, she grabbed her shirt tentatively and sniffed. It smelled in a couple places, but there wasn't anything she could do about that. She had nothing else. She readjusted her clothes and eased off the bed, a fear of the unknown holding her back, but she tried ruthlessly to wrestle it into submission.

To distract herself, she focused on her rescuer. He'd said "embee-un" when he opened his eyes, not that she had a clue what that meant. It was the only thing she'd been able to parse out. It felt like maybe a greeting?

After a few steps, she peeked through the doorway into a hall. To the right, the hallway carried on into darkness. To the left, the sound of footsteps and soft clatters drifted to her. She followed the sounds. The hallway grew lighter as she progressed until she found herself in a kitchen. A tall table sat in the middle of the room. Her savior busily moved from the back wall, which held compartments he kept reaching into, to the table, which he set items on.

The small but functional room held little else. She suspected cooking apparati waited among the compartments, but she couldn't tell by looking at them what they might be. Again, long lights lit the room. Emma crossed to the table and climbed on the tall stool. She felt like a toddler trying to climb on a chair. Her feet dangled in the air, and she looked up, taking in the unusual architecture.

Like the other room, the walls were smooth except for intricate carvings, but now she realized that unlike human habitations, the walls sloped into the ceiling, and a large skylight covered most of the space above. With the skylight illuminated by the wall lights, she could just barely see its surface. Too coarse to be glass, could it be some form of stone? Quartz and diamond on Earth were fairly opaque when cut right.

He nudged her arm, and she looked over at him. Grabbing her hands, he examined her wrists, nodding in approval before kneeling and grabbing her feet.

Oh right.

As if to remind her, her ankles started throbbing as he peeled the bandages away and stood moments later. Seemingly satisfied, he pointed to a dish sitting in front of her, laden with what looked like food. As if she were dense, he pointed at his mouth to indicate she should eat. "Aya."

She scowled, but looked down at the plate again. It was rather beautiful. Rectangular, and more of a mix between a tray and a bowl, she suspected it was made of the same trees she'd seen since landing here. The wood was pale, lighter than pine and almost white in color, except for the deep purple striations she suspected had to be the tree's rings.

The offerings on the tray were equally appealing. A variety of fruits or vegetables in the most vibrant colors she'd ever seen sat on the left side of the tray, all cut into nice, edible pieces. On the right were slices of a deep brown, almost black bread with light colored seeds in it for contrast. The bread looked dense and hearty, and she pinched off a piece and bit into it, moaning as it touched her tongue. Bloody Hell, that was good. She picked up an entire slice and bit half of it off, then reached for the nearest fruit and put it in her mouth with the bread, wondering if it would add or detract from the flavor.

Emma moaned again when the lightly sweet fruit met the darker taste of the bread. She wanted to tell him how good his food was, but didn't know how. After all, even on Earth, some words and gestures had vastly different meanings in different cultures. She looked up from her food, but needn't have worried. It seemed her wildly exaggerated enjoyment of her food had not gone unnoticed.

Apparently, some things *were* universal.

———

Beeyun sat wide-eyed as his brave one enjoyed her food, shoveling bites into her pink mouth with fervor. He couldn't believe she moaned so enthusiastically eating a simple piece of bread. He sat across from her, starting in on his own food when his brother's voice called from the entrance. His brave one squeaked and jumped in her seat, her eyes going wide and her body tense.

"Tsu," he said in a soothing tone, holding out his hand to stay her in her seat.

She calmed, watching him intently for a moment before turning her head toward the voice. His chest felt warm at the faith she gave him.

"I'm in the kitchen," he called out.

His brother's footfalls echoed off the walls, and in moments, he walked through the kitchen doorway. Anan almost stumbled as his gaze caught on the woman across from Beeyun.

"She is my guest," Beeyun said, uncomfortable with the idea of his brother seeing her as dangerous or hostile.

Anan nodded slowly. "What is she?" He said it in the same tone someone might use when encountering a slathering beast with gnashing teeth.

Beeyun flinched, but answered anyway. "I'm not sure yet. Her and her people landed here two days ago."

"Landed here?" Anan seemed incredulous.

Beeyun spoke up before his brother started in on some tirade. "They landed on my territory in some big metal flying beast. I've never seen anything like it."

"I'd like to see it."

Beeyun stiffened but nodded and started shoveling food in his mouth.

"Aya," his brave one said, looking at his brother, but pointing to the food. Was she asking him to eat with them? Did she understand that much?

"Don't mind if I do," Anan said, smiling hesitantly at her and taking a seat. The tension had dropped from his body. He grabbed for a piece of bread, watching her for a moment more before turning to Beeyun. "I can see why you brought her home. She's charming."

"And hardworking and brave." Everything he'd always strived to be.

"Oh?"

"She ran straight into the forest after a pyor explosion to help her fellows."

"Brave or foolish."

"Brave. It is not the only example, just the best."

Anan nodded. "And the others?"

Beeyun frowned. "They are… hakkan." He knew no other word for it. Hakkan… their word for anyone or anything that was careless with nature's gifts. It was among the most terrible of insults and the worst thing one could say about someone in his culture.

Anan frowned, the tension returning. "What have they done?"

"You will see, but they have also disrupted the maenu, so we should not get too close." Though, enough time had passed since the fire. It was probably safe, but one could never be too careful with maenu.

Anan gasped, half choking on the huge wad of bread in his mouth. "Good Goddess, please tell me they are not hostile."

Beeyun frowned, which was answer enough.

Anan turned to the woman again.

Beeyun knew what was going through his brother's head. "She is innocent."

"I very much doubt it."

Beeyun leaned forward, gazing hard at his brother, feeling protective of her. "I saved her from her people."

Anan jerked his head back around to face his brother. "How so?"

"The maenu had been affecting them badly." Beeyun frowned. "Though, now that I think of it, it didn't seem to affect her at all." He looked at his brave one, puzzled by that peculiarity. "They tied her up and were circling her. I could feel the malicious energy coming off them. I didn't know what they would do, but felt she did not deserve whatever fate they'd decided on for her."

Anan nodded and sighed. "I'm sure I would have done the same in your place. Come, you've finished your food. Let's go see your intruders."

Beeyun nodded, grabbed the trays, and dusted them off, placing them in the steam oven. He walked around the table, patted his guest on the shoulder reassuringly, then followed his brother out.

Emma felt like a painting on the wall or something. Throughout the entire conversation, she hadn't understood a single word, and with the number of times they'd looked at her, she felt certain they were talking about her.

In the beginning, she'd said the one word she actually knew, wanting to contribute at least a little, but after that, she felt like her eyes would glaze over at the rapid-fire manner they spewed sentences back and forth. Then she just focused on expressions and body language. Something was definitely bothering them, though they smiled most times when they looked at her, so she didn't think they held any ill will toward her.

Then the two left with barely any acknowledgement of her presence, though what could they honestly say? Body language only went so far, and she supposed the pat on the shoulder was at least something. As she finished popping the last of her food in her mouth, she wondered where they were off to. What were they doing? What had them so bothered?

With the last of her food finished, she picked up her tray and walked around the table. She'd seen him put his tray in one of the cabinets on the wall, but which one? Everything was so alien. Even the table and chairs were just strange enough to leave her feeling like more of a pet than a guest. The chairs were too tall, the table almost came to her shoulders. All the building materials were natural. She suspected their society had technology, but she didn't see it, didn't recognize it.

She liked her alien, had felt at home with him, but now that he was gone, she just felt listless, uncertain, useless and out of place. Everything was ill suited for her and she understood none of it. Even so, she was more comfortable in this completely alien environment than she'd ever been back with the other humans. They'd strung her up, for crying out loud! "What the fuck!" she said to no one, waving the dirty tray she'd forgotten she carried.

Right, task at hand.

Emma started at the right and moved her way left across the wall of cabinets, searching for the one her alien had used. Since she also wanted to learn her environment, she took her time, methodically checking the entire kitchen area. The first cabinet contained a top shelf with baskets of silverware—some similar to human utensils, others so strange she couldn't hope to fathom their usage. The bottom shelf held trays much larger than the ones he'd taken out today. She found trays identical to the one in her hand in the next cabinet. They sat stacked in perfect piles, only slightly wobbly because they weren't uniform. Probably handmade.

As she stepped in front of a taller compartment, she could feel the difference. It radiated heat. She tilted the lid up—a thin piece of stone with two wooden handles at the front—and spotted the tray he'd deposited. Steam basked her face in heat, causing her to sweat and shift her face to the side. It must be like a dishwasher. She carefully placed the tray inside and closed the lid.

The next cabinet was equally warm with an identical cover. She tilted this cover up too, and dry heat blasted her in the face. For drying? Or maybe it was an oven. She looked a little closer, her engineer's brain whirring to life. What was supplying the heat? She didn't see any gas lines or power cords. The cabinets were flush to the wall and floor. Could it be geothermal? She couldn't imagine making an oven or dish-washer out of geothermal energy, but what other options were there? She couldn't see enough of how it worked to figure it out.

It was all fascinating. Living on a farm, they'd had to be somewhat self-sustaining. Geothermal, solar panels, a small garden out back to feed the household. She'd spent more time harvesting from the garden and doing repairs as a child than learning for school. By the time she'd entered pilot training after her engineering degree, she could take apart, repair, and put back together any item on the farm. The temptation was huge to try to figure out how everything worked here, to understand it. Surrounded by all these strange things she couldn't comprehend, that were clearly designed for people much taller than her, she felt even more of an outsider than she did before.

Emma hugged herself and moved on in her exploration, though it didn't have the same appeal it once did. The last few cabinets were filled with food—fruit, bread, flour, what looked like seasonings, and other staples. So where did he keep the perishables? There certainly wasn't anything resembling a refrigerator or cold box in the kitchen.

Emma turned around and made a left at the entrance to the kitchen. She quickly passed the bedroom on the right and kept going. Darkness consumed her, but within moments she exited into the first rays of dawn. The early morning light leaked through the trees in front of her, illuminating the gentle incline of the mountain the alien's home was carved from. From the outside, it looked like the entrance to a cave. She ran her hands over the rough surface around the entrance. Cool rock scraped against her palm. "Neat." She moved closer to the entrance, running her hand over the opening. "Huh." It was too smooth, carved. Someone had built this home just as they would have on Earth, only here he chose to make his home blend into the environment. Emma would have never found it if she'd been traveling through the forest.

She didn't wander any farther from the entrance, keeping her hand firmly against the stone. Looking behind her at the dark, forbidding forest, Emma knew full well what could happen to a person who wandered onto unfamiliar territory, and Earth didn't even have the dangers this planet did.

With a final longing glance at daylight, Emma reentered the "house," intent on exploring in the opposite direction. Her hand rested on her small pack like a security blanket, the only thing other than her clothes she still had. She passed the kitchen and slipped into a room on the right. This room sloped down immediately upon entering, leading to what resembled a toilet and the biggest inlaid tub she'd ever heard of. She reached down and dipped her hands in the water, closing her eyes in pleasure at how the warm water caressed her digits. "Wow."

Emma opened her eyes again, watching the water with fascination as she twirled her fingers along the surface. The sound of water rushing and bubbling filled the room, but there were no spigots, no drain that she could see. It appeared naturally replenishing, which meant there had to be a hot spring nearby. Her eyes lit up at the thought. So that was how the oven worked! Of course! The engineer in her did a little dance. The residence must have been planned over a natural hot spring, which produced enough steam to heat both cabinets. Brilliant!

She smiled at her discovery, intrigued by the simple ingenuity of the local species. Standing up, she resumed her search. It took a few minutes, and a winding curve off to the right, but finally the temperature started to drop. Emma rubbed her arms and soon found herself in a room deep in the house. Stone shelves were carved from the walls, and all manners of foodstuffs and containers littered them. Well, that explained the lack of an ice box. Of course, he wouldn't need an appliance if he lived in a cave.

Beeyun squatted down next to Anan, allowing the vegetation to serve as his cover. The chaotic energy he'd felt the last time he came to this meadow had not abated, and he suspected it would be some time before the effects of the maenu wore off completely. While burning it released most of it at once, giving it a more aggressive effect, it also drastically reduced how long it remained in the environment.

It had been a risk rescuing his brave one last night. He could have been affected by the maenu himself, but he'd held his breath as he ran through the field, hoping he could reach the other side before needing oxygen. But he couldn't just leave her there, not with these people. He looked back at the meadow.

Here and there, the foreign people sported skin discolorations similar in tone to his own skin. The people yelled in their alien tongue, their body language telling more than anything else. Someone swung a fist, and a fight broke out. The fight grew, people joining the fray as if it were a party they couldn't wait to join.

"Do you understand any of their language yet?" Anan asked, focusing on the task at hand.

He tapped his ear where his translation implant resided. "No. I haven't sampled enough speech to get a rudimentary grammar system and vocabulary base yet." He didn't know a ton about the implant, didn't know when it would start translating for him, but it had to be soon, right?

Anan nodded. "They're a savage bunch, aren't they? I've never seen someone respond to the maenu that severely before."

To be fair, how often did their people stumble into the maenu? And how many of them would be stupid enough to not only stumble upon it, but set up camp in it? Or land that great beast in it? Or set fire to it? "You have to admit, they've had more exposure than any creature on this planet is likely to. We know better."

Anan chuckled, leaning back against a tree to look his brother in the eye. "Yes, of course." His expression turned serious. "Do you think they're dangerous?"

"At the moment, certainly. Without being under the influence? I'm not sure. They're certainly hakkan, but that doesn't make them dangerous."

Anan nodded, looking over his shoulder at the mess the aliens had made. "We need to do something about this."

"I've been trying." And he would continue trying. He *would* drive them away. He just needed to figure out the best approach. He needed a new plan. "They're a resilient bunch, I'll give them that."

Anan scowled at him. "You should have told me. I could have handled this. It's my job."

Beeyun stiffened, pride getting the better of him. "This is my territory and my responsibility." He'd been entrusted with ensuring its natural beauty while providing their people with the resources it supplied so generously. It was an important role, passed down to so few in their society. To say he could not care for the land? How could his brother ever *think* that?

But did he really expect anything less? He'd always lived in his brother's shadow. And he'd received his position by birth, not by merit. At the rate he was going, he would never live up to his namesake.

"I apologize. You're right, but while you are my brother, I am the leader of our people. This is my responsibility just as much as yours."

Feeling stupid for his outburst, Beeyun looked away. It was always Beeyun's fault, wasn't it?

"Don't worry. I'll have men here inside of a couple days to wipe their presence off your lands."

Panic gripped Beeyun. "No." He shook his head, centering himself. Where was this panic coming from? "I don't think that's such a good idea." But why? He couldn't think. Wouldn't it be best if they drove them off sooner than later?

Anan just raised an eyebrow, waiting for an explanation.

Beeyun scrambled for something to say. "We don't know why they're here, how they discovered this place, what their intentions are. We don't know that if we sent them away, they wouldn't just come back with reinforcements, cause even more destruction." Not to mention, he would have to send his brave one away as well. He didn't relish the thought. What would happen to her if she returned to her people, the same people who'd tied her up? "Best for us to gather intelligence before we act." It would give him time to come up with a plan. He *needed* a plan.

Anan smiled. "You've always been the wise one, Beeyun. Maybe you should have been named that?"

He flinched. "I am brave, too."

"I know. Otherwise, I wouldn't be entrusting this task to you. I know you have the heart to see it through to the end. Be safe, brother." Anan grasped his brother's shoulder, then stood to walk away.

CHAPTER ELEVEN

*B*y the time her alien returned later that day, Emma had explored every inch of his cave home and was bored to tears. She'd never realized how much she relied on the little conveniences of her society. Tablet computers. Cell phones. Heck, she even used a smartwatch to keep track of her exercise and listen to music back on Earth. How had she become such a slave to her devices?

So when she saw him enter the kitchen, she lit up, nearly falling out of her chair in glee.

He smiled back and said something she assumed was a greeting.

"Hi." She waved her fingers at him, feeling like a teenage girl and totally foolish. What was wrong with her?

He made some hand gestures she didn't understand, then pulled some food out of the cabinets, putting them on the table. He waved at the food. "Ayan."

She frowned, but leaned forward, curious about what he had in mind. He'd said "aya" before, which she'd assumed meant eat. Did he want her to eat? But then, why say it that way?

What was different? Did he mean something else? "Ah-ayan? Food?" It would make sense. She'd never been big on language, preferring to work with her hands, but it made sense that food and eat would sound similar, right?

He beamed a smile at her, nodding his head. He picked up a fruit thing. "Soo-at."

"Soo-at, fruit?" She pointed at the round, fist-sized, red thing.

"Ka-ov." He held up the dark bread from earlier.

"Ka-of. Bread?" Was this a language lesson? Was he trying to teach her how to speak with him?

This time, he pointed at himself, then his mouth, like gesturing to eat. "Ayi." He pointed to Emma. "Aya." Lastly, he pointed at both of them. "Ayiu."

Yup, definitely a language lesson.

She smirked, looking forward to picking up some vital skills. "I eat. You eat. We eat." She followed his motions, picking up on the conjugations. Hopefully, the language wouldn't have non-standard conjugations. Those had always screwed her up when learning Spanish. And there were parts of the English language she *still* couldn't quite grasp.

He smiled at her again. She couldn't imagine he understood her translations any better than she understood him. Though, it was nice that he was trying to teach her. She wanted to learn. She wanted to talk to him. Why had he saved her? Why did she feel so comfortable with him? She couldn't even speak to him, but she felt more at ease in his company than she had in anyone's in her entire life.

Although, maybe the lack of communication was part of it. Maybe it gave her free license to be herself. He wouldn't judge her based on societal norms, and he didn't have a clue what she was saying. They had no expectations of each other. They could just *be*…

By the end of the day, they'd wandered the entire house, pointing at objects, speaking names for things, and going over conjugations of verbs. It didn't take long for her to realize most verbs had an associated noun. Or that verbs always ended in vowels, nouns in consonants. Strangely, all past and future conjugations were accomplished by adding a word before the verb—no for past and ya for future tense.

It was really a very simple language, thank God, but elegant in its simplicity. It made English seem clunky and awkward. Over the course of the day, she'd put together enough vocabulary to express all her basic needs in his language. She wasn't sure she could have accomplished that with a language from Earth. And having that knowledge made her feel more secure, more confident, less isolated. The language barrier didn't feel like as much of a wall anymore.

And they'd even exchanged names. Beeyun, his name was Beeyun. It reminded her of what he'd said to her the morning after they first met. Embee-un, wasn't it? She wondered if his name meant something. With what she'd learned thus far, she suspected it did.

It also made her think of those first encounters. She remembered touching his face for the first time, him kissing her, watching him in his sleep, him kissing her forehead. She rubbed her lips, thinking of the plan she'd formed while he was gone today. It was probably a bad idea. She was running on little sleep, but she just couldn't get her attraction to him out of her head, and it just seemed like a missed opportunity if she didn't at least *try* to act on it.

Unfortunately, he'd been completely disciplined all day. She'd occasionally seen what she thought might be interest in his eyes, but he'd done nothing untoward. In fact, he treated her like she was too good for him, which was sweet, but a little frustrating.

Now or never, Emma.

She crooked her finger at him, hoping she wasn't making a complete ass of herself. "Tuva an, Beeyun." Tuva was a weird verb in that, from what she could tell, it meant anything referring to movement. So, tuva an meant come here, and tuva ov meant go there. She liked the economy and simplicity of it, and it certainly made it easier when there weren't a thousand ways of saying the same thing.

Taking a deep breath, she smiled, but didn't have the guts to make it seductive.

I really don't know what the hell I'm doing here.

Beeyun followed her with a confused look on his face.

They took a right turn and started the downward descent into the bathroom. Her heart leapt a little in her chest, thinking of the wonderful tub she hadn't tried yet. She planned to do that now.

"Tuva an," she said again when they reached the edge of the tub.

The heat from the water steamed around them, making her sweat under her clothes. Or maybe it was her own thoughts getting the best of her? She glanced up into his eyes and frowned. He still looked confused, though now a bead of sweat formed on his forehead before trickling down his temple. That wasn't what she wanted to see.

She ran a hand against the closure of her shirt, her nerves rising to choke her.

What the hell am I doing? Maybe I should just walk away, pretend this never happened.

She could easily see herself fleeing and hiding under blankets in the bedroom, but what would that solve? That was no way to live.

Emma took another deep breath and dropped her gaze to his chest, unable to do this and look him in the eye. She started stripping, the loss of clothing a welcome relief in the sweltering heat. It really was too hot in here to be wearing any.

As she was reaching for her pants, he touched her chin, tilting her head up. She froze. The confusion was gone from his gaze. Now, fire simmered from deep within. Her breath caught in her chest, and she forgot how to use her hands.

Suddenly, he picked her up and jumped into the water. Shocked out of her daze, she laughed as hot water splashed against her overheated skin. She didn't remember getting fully undressed, but skin met skin as they settled into the water, giving her the confidence she needed to act. Reaching out, she grabbed his chin and kissed him, more a need than a want in that moment. He dived into the kiss, but soon enough started migrating.

"Beeyun," she gasped as he nibbled her ear. His name felt good on her lips, so she repeated it when he reached her breasts. "Beeyun."

She grabbed at his hair, tugging him closer as they sunk into the water. He seemed determined to get comfortable, and Emma was happy to oblige.

For all of thirty seconds, and then she started getting antsy, squirming for more, begging for an end, something. She reached and found him under the water. He gasped, burying his face in her hair.

He murmured something she didn't recognize, then surged into her.

Emma groaned something that might have been a yes or his name. She wasn't sure. Her brain wasn't exactly running on all cylinders right now.

It felt like heaven, though. The warm water made her feel like she was floating on a sensual cloud, and the connection made her feel like she was right where she belonged for once. She looked down and smiled at the contrast of purple skin flowing into her own tan skin.

He lifted her hips, and she watched in fascination as his body disappeared into hers. Something about it compelled her, made her want to watch again and again. It made her even more aroused just thinking about it. She wished she could tell him how beautiful he was, but she didn't have the words.

So, instead, she kissed him, filling the expression with all the passion and emotion she felt. She didn't know what was happening, how things would end up, but she'd never felt more alive, more connected to a person, in her life. And it only seemed to be getting stronger. She didn't want to leave.

Time stopped, and she hovered on a precipice. Her entire body strained for what waited on the other side. She pulled at his hair as it became more and more unbearable. He laughed and trailed his lips down her throat again while his hands wandered south.

"Mava am," he whispered in her ear. She didn't know the word, but the way his breath coasted across her skin did it for her. She soared, her body spasming around him only moments before he gave up the ghost himself.

Emma floated on the high for a while, enjoying the way the water buoyed her, the way Beeyun's hands ran soothing circles on her back.

This was a really good idea.

Beeyun felt at peace, like all was right with the world. Emma rested her head against his chest, her smaller frame making it impossible to reach his face with them still joined as they were. It felt wonderful, and he wrapped his arms around her, keeping her tight against him. He would love to be inside this woman for all of time, but it soon became clear she wasn't in the same state of mind. She started wiggling, shifting on his lap as if she was trying to separate from him. Beeyun sighed. It was rare for a Danaus female to want to separate immediately after sex, and it usually meant she wasn't satisfied.

For a few moments, she had rested contentedly against his chest, sated and lethargic, but it hadn't lasted long. He tried to remind himself that she wasn't Danaus, that he shouldn't apply the same labels and logic that he would to one of his own kind. They still had a language barrier between them, and he couldn't read her mind. It ate at him. He didn't know what the problem was. Maybe it wasn't his failing at all. Maybe she was uncomfortable with their intimacy now that they weren't in the heat of the act. Or maybe men didn't have the stamina to last on her world? He wished they shared a few words that could help, but some things were hard to teach… and he was no teacher.

He sighed and lifted her up off him. With having just come, it wasn't an easy task. He'd swelled after release, effectively locking them together. He suspected there was some biological advantage to it, but he didn't know what. What he *did* know was it was a matter of pride to stay within a female for as long as possible after sex.

Beeyun gasped a little as her body finally released him. He settled her back atop his thighs and pulled her into his arms. If he couldn't be inside her, this was the next best thing.

"Tsu," he said, continuing to rub her back, trying to soothe her. He needed to tear down this language barrier. The lessons today had definitely helped, giving them a good baseline of words, and she'd repeated each word in her own language, allowing his implant to work faster to build a database.

Beeyun leaned against the hard stone of the bath as steam from the hot spring pervaded the room. Splashing sounds surrounded them as little movements from his brave one displaced the water. She made little contented sounds as she cuddled up to him, putting his mind at ease and allowing him to focus on what to do next.

He stared at the stone wall behind Emma's head, his fingers brushing over the ends of her hair as he started each stroke down her back. He liked that gentle sensation. It grounded his thoughts. He needed to continue the language lessons, but he also needed to monitor her people. He also needed to check his implant, see how far it had come, if there was anything he could do to speed it along.

More than anything, he wanted to talk with his brave one. He would do almost anything for that.

DAY 8

It didn't take long for Emma to wish she had something to write with. The next morning, he started bright and early trying to teach her more words, and her head was near to exploding with the information. She was already overwhelmed with the new clothes his friend had brought, which didn't fit right, feeling tight or pulling in odd places. Still, it was better than wearing her clothes for the third day in a row. Before she'd even finished her meal, she was starting to lose track of his lesson. Still sitting at the table, she made a scribbling motion in the air, hoping he might understand, putting a lot of faith in that hope.

But Beeyun nodded, standing and reaching up to the skylight above his head. He removed something from a holder on the ceiling, and she realized the skylight was larger than she'd thought. Whatever he handed her had been blocking part of it. Made of something slick as glass, she wondered how to use it. Whatever it was, it was paper thin, made of stone, and warmed her palms from sitting in the heat of the sun.

Beeyun leaned over and tapped the surface. Emma didn't know what to expect, but when he then ran his finger over it, a line drew across the pale surface of the "stone." It had an attached stylus, and she drew it across the surface, her eyes going wide as a thick line followed the point. Then Beeyun swiped his finger from the top of the surface, and a menu appeared. Emma couldn't understand a single word on the screen, but she recognized a computer menu when she saw one.

She lifted it higher in the air, looking for evidence of how it was made. It looked like a single sheet of rock until she paid a little closer attention to the back of the device. *Are those solar panels?* It didn't look like anything she'd ever seen before, but it would make sense considering where he'd stored it. Looking him in the eye once more, his race rose even higher in her esteem.

With a few gestures, he showed her how to erase mistakes, save her progress, and scroll for more open space to write. She spent the time after their meal writing down as many words as she could remember. Beeyun made it harder by constantly interrupting her either by teaching her new words or quizzing her on the words he'd already taught her.

It was exhausting, and she was almost grateful when he kissed her on the forehead, said something she suspected meant see you later, and left the cave for God only knew where.

———

Beeyun smiled as he left home. They'd made good progress since his brave one woke—both in teaching his language and learning her own. Emma, she'd called herself. Such a simple name, and yet it rolled off his tongue, made him want to say it again and again. "Emma."

With a shake of his head, he took off into the trees at a jog, his long legs eating up the ground between his home and the meadow. It took all of a few minutes to reach it, a distance that made him very uncomfortable. When he reached the last of the trees, he settled in, almost closing his eyes in the hopes of catching more of their conversations. He hoped that between the words he'd learned from Emma and what he'd overheard here, he could learn their language *and* their intentions.

He settled in against a tree, deep in the shadows, but close enough to hear. Their words washed over him, disjointed and jarring. They moved through the meadow with an edge that hadn't left yet, even after the maenu burned. Were they still affected or was something else bothering them?

After a while, even the erratic behavior of the strangers couldn't keep his focus, and his mind started to wander. Specifically, it wandered to Emma. Why had he been so resistant to the idea of sending her home? He knew that was best for her and his people, and yet his mind balked at the idea.

Was it just loneliness? He'd spent so many of his years alone in his home, on his lands. Beeyun had passed it off as being fastidious, protecting and tending his lands, but deep down he knew he was lying to himself. But while he could admit that he'd lied to himself for years, the truth of the current situation eluded him.

He knew he respected Emma, wanted the best for her, and didn't trust her people. She wouldn't be safe with them. Was that it? Beeyun shook himself. She wasn't his responsibility, no matter how much he wished it were so. He wanted to protect her. He wanted to provide for her, keep her safe. It was madness. Emma wasn't Danaus. She didn't belong here. She never would. He couldn't keep her.

She's not a pet…

His mind looped over and over the topic like a predator circling its prey, waiting for an opening. None came, and by the time he stood to return to his Emma, he'd really only come to one conclusion—he couldn't bear to let her go. No matter what, he needed to find a way to keep her. He had to. He couldn't imagine being without her.

West was torn. He stood next to the *Endeavour*, his back pressed against the contoured metal. In spite of the day's warmth, the ship was cool to the touch, causing a chill to race through his body intermittently.

It had been days since their pilot was taken. He couldn't get the image of her being ripped from that beam out of his head. It had seemed like nothing more than a streak of purple as the crowd gathered around her, thirsty for blood.

It left him pulled in two directions. On the one side, every time he thought of their pilot, it reminded him of every time she countermanded him or thwarted his authority, which pissed him off. On the other, some deep, whisper-quiet, part of him kept reminding him they needed her, though the tension in his body made it hard to think through why.

He needed to do something, though. Tensions were only getting worse. Another fight broke out, shouts filling the field. West pushed off the ship and ran into the fray, determined to put an end to it, but it wasn't so easy.

When he arrived, the fight had grown, pulling in anyone nearby. A half-dozen people now threw limbs at each other, creating a flailing mass of kinetic energy ready to connect with anything and everything. West pulled one person away, throwing them to the ground outside the chaotic mob, but then a fist connected with his cheek, sending pain shooting through his face and blanking out his thoughts.

A moment was all it took. He reacted, swinging out with his own punch that landed hard, jarring his entire arm, and he was lost.

<hr>

Emma woke to Beeyun kissing her temple, his lips feathering over her skin. He murmured something to her, followed by her name, but her sleep-addled brain couldn't decipher the foreign words. Daylight still glowed from the skylights, but that hadn't stopped exhaustion from dragging at her when Beeyun didn't return.

As she started to wake some more, she registered how his hand lightly petted her, just running in gentle strokes down her skin. She wanted to ask him where he'd gone, what he'd been doing, but even if she could figure out what to say, she didn't think she would understand his response.

Besides, even if she didn't want to admit it, she had a nagging feeling she knew *exactly* where he'd gone—the meadow where she'd parked the ship. *Emma* might have chosen to forget about it, but she doubted he had. *Someone* had been terrorizing their settlement. Deep down, some part of her knew it was him. Had he destroyed more buildings? Had he hurt anyone?

The second question seemed ludicrous even the moment it popped into her head. He hadn't once hurt anyone, even when any human probably would have. While her people had been at each other's throats, he'd still been doing strictly property damage.

She grabbed his hand on an upstroke, bringing it in front of her face as she opened her eyes. Splaying his fingers wide, she traced her fingers over the contours, wondering how the claws formed. She'd seen the buildings, even seen his claws that first day right before they'd kissed, but she hadn't seen them since. Could he be like the shape-shifters back home? Or maybe his people were like the Incirrina, who could only change certain parts of their bodies at will?

Or maybe he was like a cat, with retractable claws? That would be the simplest solution, right? She ran her hands over his fingers. They looked so similar to her own. She felt nothing that might be a retracted claw. How did they work?

Emma paused, realizing what she'd done again. She held his hand, rubbing back and forth. She'd been thinking about the others, thinking about the damage done, and then she'd immediately lost herself in thoughts of Beeyun… again.

What is wrong *with you?*

She couldn't look at him as her thoughts ran in circles, spinning out of control. Why was she acting like this? Sure, she felt at home with him, comfortable in a way she never had before. And while she'd only seen one other of his kind, a man she still didn't know the name of, that small connection made her feel more anchored than ever before. It gave her hope that he was part of a larger community, a community that she could be part of, too.

She liked that idea, but maybe a bit too much. Could she really find a place here? She was another species, other, different. She was different here in ways she'd never been back home. Emma couldn't hide her differences here. She would always be that weird little alien.

Except Beeyun never treated her like that. He treated her with respect. And even the other man, the only other alien she'd met, didn't treat her badly. He'd seemed hostile at first, but who wouldn't be? He didn't know her, didn't know what she wanted or was capable of. Of course, he would be suspicious. But it hadn't lasted long. Before he'd even started eating, he'd begun treating her amicably. She remembered thinking how different that was to humans. She couldn't imagine any human warming to someone so quickly.

And without even language to smooth the edges? She couldn't speak to him, after all. She'd said one word, asking him to eat. That was it, but he'd still smiled at her, relaxed.

Emma looked up at Beeyun finally, hope and excitement sprouting in her chest, growing. She was learning to communicate with him. Someday, she felt confident they would be able to speak to one another. Really communicate.

Someday, they could have a real relationship.

Was that what she wanted?

Was this where she *really* belonged?

Beeyun wanted more than anything for the language barrier between them to be gone. He wanted to know what she was thinking. He *always* wanted to know what she was thinking. Probably, the very fact that he couldn't ask and she couldn't tell made that need all the more acute.

He sat on the edge of his bed, the surface dipping under his heavy weight. His hand itched to run across her face once more, but she held it in an iron grip. Her hands felt tiny wrapped around his, like a child holding onto a parent. His other hand held him upright on the bed, flexing into the spongy material. She still lay wrapped in blankets and wearing some thin nightdress.

She's so fragile.

The thought would hit him out of the blue. Most of the time, he would forget, not even noticing the more glaring differences like her hair and skin color. But every once in a while, it would hit him like a punch to the chest. This woman, this beautiful, courageous woman who could make him forget with the very force of her personality, was tiny, fragile by his people's standards. He'd seen how easily the others were injured in their skirmishes. Sometimes, he feared he could hurt her, break her, by accident.

And yet she explored his world without fear. As he looked down at the hand she still held, the hand she stared so intently at, he wondered what it would take to protect her, to keep her. And would she let him, because he very much doubted such a strong personality would take kindly to being seen as fragile.

He chuckled and shook his head. She would probably hit him if she knew, and that was part of the reason he loved her.

CHAPTER TWELVE

Things had gone from bad to worse since a purple streak had taken Lacy's friend away. She and her family had moved into Emma's quarters afterward. It was the only place in the ship with both beds and a lock on the door. She didn't trust her fellow crew-members, and neither did her wife, Rick.

She looked out the SmartGlass for the thousandth time in the days since Emma's disappearance. Simultaneously missing her friend and thanking the heavens the woman was out of harm's way, she'd found herself searching the tree line as she'd so often found Emma doing. Looking back, it was almost as if Emma *knew* something else was out there.

Now, Lacy just spent her time in the pilot's chair, staring out at the trees, searching for a shade of purple that didn't quite belong. Of course, maybe the blur she'd seen had been clothing, in which case her looking for a purple shape was hopeless.

Still, she hoped someone was out there. Or something. She hoped Emma was safe, that she'd been rescued. Anymore, she didn't even recognize the people she'd spent so many months with traveling to this planet. It was as if they'd been possessed.

Really, she felt like a leading lady in a horror movie about body snatching aliens or something. It would fit just as well as the next theory.

Emma being taken had sent them into a frenzy of sorts. The fights had dwindled, but the madness remained. More and more, she heard whispers about "The Beast." Some talked about retribution, even though they'd all wanted The Beast to take her, hurt her, maybe even kill her. They'd intended to make Emma a sacrifice, but now those same people acted as if they needed to avenge her.

Others seemed to have completely devolved, turning into little more than animals. Territorial, aggressive, fighting over food. Lacy never felt safe outside these walls anymore. She didn't know what someone might do, who she might encounter.

"I'm hungry," Jacie whined, rubbing her stomach with a frown on her face.

Lacy turned around, keeping her voice low so Rick wouldn't wake up. "Okay, sweetie. I'll get you something from the mess hall. Be right back." Since there were only two beds in the room, both of them exceptionally small, they'd decided to sleep in shifts. It wasn't ideal, but it was better than the alternative.

Apprehension filled her as she unlocked the door and slipped out, hyperaware of her surroundings, probably uncomfortably close to how a soldier assessed his surroundings before entering hostile territory. Closing the door, relief rushed through her like a bunch of knots untying as the door's lock engaged with an audible clank. Her family was safe so long as that door remained locked.

Using her ears as much as her eyes to guide her, she made her way to the mess hall where food waited to feed her bottomless pit of a daughter. She smiled, but that didn't stop her from listening to how sound carried across the ship's interior. Because of the predominantly metal construction, hopefully she would have ample warning of another nearby.

Still, as the hall loomed in front of her, horror movies came to mind again. Wasn't there always some seemingly empty hallway the hero, or especially heroine, would have to travel, trying to stay under the radar of whatever big bad happened to plague the place? Her mind drifted to a particular scene in The Shining. Also, probably half the scenes from Deep Blue Sea. And Alien vs. Predator.

Why had her mom seen fit to educate her with almost every horror movie, good or bad, produced in the entire history of the film industry? It really left the imagination with entirely too much to contemplate in situations like this. Sometimes, ignorance was bliss, and she was anything but ignorant when it came to horror plots.

Damn, I wish I had a weapon.

Not that it would do her any good. The worst offenders were all male and all huge in comparison to her. It was like they'd devolved, slipping into a natural pecking order. The strongest could dominate the weaker males, so the scientists tended to think smarter, acting like she did, planning excursions carefully to avoid fights they knew they couldn't win.

She let out a little prayer of thanks when she reached the mess hall without having a heart attack. Or being attacked by this expedition's version of Jason Voorhees. Lacy skipped across the hall to the kitchen, grabbing a bucket she could use to carry stuff, and throwing anything and everything she could find in it. At this point, she didn't much care what they ate. She was too freaked out to linger. Her hands shook as she loaded the bin.

When the receptacle was full, she slipped out of the kitchen, trying to keep quiet while she made quick work of the floor between her and her destination.

She'd just reached the last hallway when an arm latched on, fingers digging into skin. A scream ripped from her throat, and she swung the bucket, aiming at whatever had grabbed her. It collided with a thunk, followed by a cacophony of unpleasant sounds as the foods she'd chosen hit the floor.

The man roared and seized her by the throat, slamming her back against the doorway with a speed and force that knocked the wind from her and had her seeing stars. Hard metal ground into her spine as his fingers tightened. He leaned forward, overwhelming her personal space with his ominous presence. She flailed for a moment of panic before the reality settled in—if she didn't escape, she would die. Her daughter would lose a mother.

Determination surged through her. She *needed* to escape, *needed* to get back to Rickelle and Jacie. No other result was acceptable. Her head pounded with lack of oxygen as she continued to gasp, her hands pulling at his grip, trying to separate his fingers from her flesh. It wasn't working. She couldn't break free. Her feet scrambled for traction, slamming into the wall, his legs, but it didn't stop him. He didn't react. She had to break free, had to get back to the control room.

Letting go of the death grip she'd reflexively taken of his fingers around her throat, she slipped her arms between them. He didn't even notice, his breath cascading in a hot, foul assault on her cheek. She slammed her hands into his elbows. At first, she feared they wouldn't budge, that he was too strong for her, that she was too weak. Rick had always said Lacy needed to exercise more, build up some muscle strength. Then his elbows folded outward slightly, and she pushed out hard with both arms, causing him to lose his grip and drop her.

She collapsed on her knees, air coming desperately through her raw throat. But as her thinking cleared, she knew she needed to act. She was still vulnerable. He could still get her again. She hadn't even hurt him. There was nothing to stop him from leaning down and strangling her again. Determined to escape, she reached out for the target staring her right in the face. His bits squished under her hold, and an image of a terrier dangling from its prey popped into her head, almost making her laugh. She dug in harder and twisted, finally registering the high-pitched, panicked cries coming from above her. He scratched at her hand, his short nails tearing at her skin, but she didn't let go until he collapsed to his knees. He dropped, keeling over onto his back.

Lacy let go and ran, her feet finding speeds she'd never coaxed out of them before. She slammed against the door, hating the moments it took to unlock it, her fingers missing repeatedly as she panicked. "Come on," she said, her voice shaking as much as her hands.

Then the door flew open, and she ran inside, not even realizing she was running into Rick's arms. She burst into tears as her wife hugged her, holding her together.

"Shhh," Rick said, stroking her hair and back in a slow motion that soothed her just as it always did. "What happened?"

She shook her head against her partner's chest, not ready to speak, not ready to confront what had happened. Before long, the adrenaline gave way, and the shaking changed to lethargy. She yawned, barely able to keep her eyes open.

Rick rocked her back and forth. Her wife might have her faults, but Lacy loved the way she was always there for her in moments like this. She always seemed to know the right thing to do, the right things to say. Lacy never needed to speak when she was too frazzled to think. She could just *be*.

Rick led Lacy to the bed and tucked her in, kissing her forehead as she curled up on the bed. As her brain drifted on a cloud toward sleep, the last thing she remembered hearing was her daughter.

"Mommy, I'm hungry."

"Captain?"

West turned, a group of people bearing down on him. "Yes?" He struggled to keep an even keel, his nerves shot, emotions on a hair trigger lately. He didn't understand it and didn't like how it affected his ability to do his job. West relied on his steady nature to make tough decisions in dire circumstances. But right now, he wasn't sure whatever decision he made would be the right one. He didn't trust himself anymore.

The crowd's leader stepped forward, a determined look on her face. "What are you going to do about The Beast?"

The Beast? There had been increasing grumblings about it, though there'd been fewer attacks since the pilot was taken. Of course, the loss of their pilot was a major problem that had only recently started pressing on his brain. Without her, they were stranded. If things went wrong here, they were screwed.

Also, this was only ever supposed to be a temporary assignment. He and his crew were to assist with the setup of the settlement. After that, they were heading back to Earth, leaving the colonists and scientists behind. Without her, they couldn't go home.

Hell, without her, they couldn't even operate most of the ship's systems. Even some of the doors wouldn't operate without her codes. He didn't have them, had never bothered to learn them. The system was old, and he'd never used this model before. Besides, it wasn't his job to operate the ship. That was on the pilot, the pilot currently missing or dead.

His gut churned. Shit, he hoped she wasn't dead.

"Captain?"

"Yes, sorry." He shook his head, letting the smell of burnt vegetation clear his mind. He needed to stop doing that. Even when he wasn't being hijacked by his emotions, his mind would wander helplessly. It was alarming. "The Beast, right." They needed their pilot back. That was a fact.

He glanced over the crowd again. They were all a bit worse for wear. Most wore clothes smudged with dirt or soot, while some had cuts or blood stains on theirs. More than a few sported prominent bruises and one had an eye swollen shut, the swelling so bad it looked like he didn't have any eyelashes.

Really, there was only one option. They needed to get their pilot back. "We find them. Hunt them down and retrieve our pilot."

One way or another.

It was hard to focus, but a single hot drive pushed him forward. Hours ago, he and the rest of the security team had entered the trees, determined to find the beast that had been ravaging their settlement since their arrival and kill it. The almost painful press of his rifle against his shoulder kept him in control, kept him grounded.

He hated this damned planet. Nothing had gone right since they arrived, and he hadn't been able to think straight in days. Right now, he just wanted to hit something, beat it to a pulp until nothing remained but sludge. He wanted to scream. He needed to release the tension in his body, but he had a job to do. The captain had been perfectly clear. They needed to eliminate the threat and, hopefully, find their pilot.

He could have done without the second half of that directive, but he was a soldier. He followed orders. The captain deemed the pilot important, so he would do as he was told. Still, the blind rage made it hard to think and see in the dim light of the forest. He knew there were dangers here, dangers beyond the beast they hunted. He couldn't forget the explosion in the woods only days ago, but the memory felt fuzzy, hard to keep in mind, to remind himself to be careful, to watch his step.

A creature howled, and he jumped, swiveling in the direction it came from.

"Did you hear that?" someone said, their voice barely carrying on the wind, but sounding just as crazed as he felt.

"Keep moving," he said.

Their prey never made a noise when it attacked. The howling was something else. His mind drifted to one of the nights he was on patrol, and his blind rage flared up once more, causing his gun arm to shake. His index finger flexed on the trigger, ready and eager to unleash hell.

My finger shouldn't be on the trigger.

It took all his effort to pull his finger off the trigger like he'd been trained to do. It was already the fifth time he'd done so.

Something needed to break soon. He felt like he was losing his damned mind.

CHAPTER THIRTEEN

"Hello, em beeyun," Beeyun said in a combination of English and his own language.

Emma closed her eyes as he kissed her forehead, basking in the feel of his soft lips against her skin even more than his endearment. Over the last week or so, they'd managed to get pretty good at communicating with each other. Every conversation—hell, every sentence—mixed the two languages in some Frankenstein's monster montage of words, but it got the meaning across just fine, which was all that mattered in the end. She'd even learned what em beeyun meant, "my brave one." It always made her smile, knowing he saw her that way.

It also made her wonder about his name. Maybe it was like Spanish names, which often reflected simple words. Like Banderas meant flag or Iglesias meant church. Then again, the same was true with Anglicized names. You had names like Smith, Baker, and such which all had connections to professions. Others were connected to places.

How had he earned his name? Was it earned or given at birth? Beeyun certainly deserved it in her mind. He'd been very brave when he ran into that crowd of angry people and saved her. He didn't have to do that, could have stood back and watched. Emma wasn't sure she could have watched, let alone done nothing, but he didn't know her. Hell, she wasn't even the same species. She imagined it was like running out into a busy street to save a dog. Some would just flinch as the dog was run over, while others would try to save it. Not everyone held other species in the same regard as their own.

Hell, just look how people had reacted over the first treaty with an alien race. The conspiracy uncovered back then was still talked about over a decade later. That group had put every human in danger with their actions, risking a treaty that had saved them during the alien invasion that followed.

As he stood from the bed, his bare skin momentarily blinded her, dragging her out of her thoughts as he reached to put some clothes on. She wanted to ask where he went every day. They'd settled into a comfortable routine. She would wake up with him beside her, they would eat, he would leave for a spell. Often when he returned, he would wake her up with creative enthusiasm.

After pulling on his shirt, he turned back to her. "Aren't you going to get out of bed?"

She tried to feign innocence. "Me? Well, honestly, how could I deny you the show?"

Beeyun sat down on the side of the bed. "By all means, I'm watching."

Emma's grin stretched across her face. When he looked at her like that, she felt just as tall as him, like she was the most important person in his universe. Still laying in bed, she let the covers slip a little, exposing just the first inches of her bare shoulders. "Oops."

He laughed, but his eyes lit up with a fire that matched the one in her gut, and she knew he couldn't, wouldn't, look away.

She traced a hand down the center of her chest, slowly taking the sheet with it. The material crept down, exposing the first traces of her cleavage.

Playfully, she frowned and looked down. "This won't do."

"No?" he said, his voice whisper thin, his body unconsciously leaning toward her.

"No." Taking the material with her, she stood, landing her feet on the opposite side of the bed from him, the side with the door. "How can you get the full show if I'm laying down?" She traced the edge of the material, working it back and forth, again and again, watching as his eyes followed the movement like a predator.

Running one hand over her curves as the other continued to hold the material, she marveled at the daring she'd developed in such a short time. An enchantress couldn't have done such a good job at enthralling Beeyun. "Are you hungry?"

He nodded.

"What are you hungry for?" Her hand made the return trip, dancing teasingly beneath her breasts.

He let out a ragged breath and leaned closer.

Emma started shifting the material, exposing her legs rather than bringing it further down her chest. "What do you want, Beeyun?"

"Don't tease me, Emma."

"But that's half the fun." She smirked, leaning forward, letting the material gape in front so he could see all the way to the promised land. "You can have me when you catch me," she whispered. Having freed her legs with that last maneuver, she dropped the cloth, dashing from the room with a laugh that trickled out of her throat like bells.

Something fell behind her, and as Beeyun said something that sounded like a curse, she guessed it was him. Did he try to jump across the bed or something?

Emma ran, her heart pounding in her chest. Her face hurt from smiling, and she barely noticed the cool air that gave her goosebumps or her bare feet slapping against the stone floors.

She reached the kitchen and was about to round the table when Beeyun caught her, lifting her into the air by an arm around her waist and burying his face in her hair. Letting out a shriek that turned into a fit of giggles, she smiled down at him when he spun her around and propped her on the table.

"You got me."

"That I did. Come here." He sought her lips in a kiss that screamed of temptation and deprivation, but really how much deprivation could a person sock away in a couple hours?

Emma leaned into the kiss, more than happy to be caught.

Anan stepped into his brother's home with the sounds of love-making serenading him. He smiled, mischief on the brain as the feminine cries increased in tempo. The sounds led him to the kitchen, where tan and purple limbs twined together. Beeyun had the alien woman on her back on the table as he pleasured her into oblivion. Still, they hadn't noticed him, too intent on their own mutual ecstasies.

It had been so long since the last time he'd done this that a thrill ran up his spine. Public sex acts weren't that uncommon, but people tended to exhibit a certain level of decorum while in the presence of nobility and especially royalty. He snuck up behind Beeyun, silent as the grave, his hands outstretched and ready.

Then, with lightning speed, he grabbed his brother's hips and pulled, attempting to separate them just as countless of his people had done since the time they'd lived in tribes. The woman looked up, saw him over Beeyun's shoulder, and screamed, trying to cover what she could of her bare skin with her hands. It didn't cover much.

With a flailing of limbs, she managed to get out from beneath Beeyun, clumsy in her panic.

"Stop!" Beeyun called as she nearly fell off the table head first. Beeyun caught her, settling her on her feet within the safety of his arms, but she pushed him away and raced out of the room. Turning to Anan, Beeyun shoved him, practically sending him into the wall. "What the hell!"

Anan's feet skidded on the stone floor. "Beeyun," he said, unsure over his normally calm and reasonable brother's reaction. What had gotten into him?

Beeyun shook his head. "I'm not dealing with you right now." Then he stormed off after the little alien.

Which left Anan alone and confused. Why would his brother act that way? It wasn't like it was the first time he'd tested his brother's prowess. They'd grown up together. They'd done the same to each other more times than he could count. It was a point of pride to be able to stay inside your woman while another was trying to pull the two apart. It gave an extra edge to the act. Why would Beeyun get upset about it now?

Emma didn't remember any of the distance between the kitchen and the bedroom. Every inch of skin blushed with embarrassment, and as she searched for clothes in vain, her anger and frustration only grew. Why the heck would anyone do such a thing?

She found a shirt and threw it on, the armor cooling some of her embarrassment and with it some of her anger as well. When she found and donned some pants, she admitted to herself she might have overreacted. "I'm a prude." The statement didn't sit well with her, but what else could she say? Probably, it was just some cultural thing she didn't understand. She knew *nothing* about Beeyun's people after all. They'd could talk, really talk, but how much could she really learn in so short a span?

"Are you all right?" Beeyun said from the doorway.

"Yeah." She waved him off. "We can talk about it later. I'm sure there was a reason he came around. You should go talk to him."

He nodded and slipped back out.

She sat down on the bed and wondered if she should join them. Was what they needed to discuss private? Would they care?

Emma decided to give them some space, but after a few minutes of tapping her fingers against her thigh, she couldn't take the boredom or the suspense. "I'm a bad, bad girl." She stood and slinked into the kitchen. The voices of the two men came to her more as noise than language as her brain failed to keep up with the speed and variety.

At the kitchen entry, she leaned in, curious, but unsure of her welcome. Of course, slinking around like some spy was worse than intruding, but she had a hard time feeling guilty about it. She'd spent so much time around them unable to understand a single word that it had warped some of how she thought. After all, it probably wasn't the first time she'd been in the room while they discussed something she shouldn't hear…

———

It took a few minutes for Emma's panicked reaction to settle in Beeyun's consciousness. In that moment, all that had mattered to him was that she was upset, had almost been hurt in her panic, and his brother had been to blame.

The walk back to the kitchen gave him time to feel shame at his reaction. He'd actually shoved his brother. While mild as violence went, it was still violence and unprecedented in their relationship. He stood in the doorway at a loss for words. "I'm sorry."

Anan looked past him, a thoughtful look on his face. "Your alien is shy?"

Beeyun looked over his shoulder even though she was nowhere in sight. "I suppose so." He turned back. "I shouldn't have acted the way I did."

Anan held up a hand, shaking his head. "You were only responding to her distress. I should have realized she might not handle it as one of our own would."

Beeyun sighed in relief. "So, what brings you here?"

"What else?"

"I have it under control." Beeyun bristled.

"Are you sure?" Anan said, skeptical.

"Yes," he said through his teeth.

Anan crossed his arms, his jaw stubborn as he stared his brother down. "They're hunting you, Beeyun. This needs to end."

Beeyun flinched, his mind blanking for a moment as his brother's words settled in. "You've been going behind my back?" He took a step forward before he could stop himself. A room still separated them, but he felt like he was a moment away from pouncing and disgracing himself even further.

Anan dropped his arms at his sides. "That's my job! I have to look after *everyone*, including you. *Everyone* is my responsibility. I've left this to you to deal with, but I can't let this go any further. I will not have one of my people attacked by invaders hopped up on maenu."

Some of the tension drained from him. "What have you done?"

"I have a contingent of soldiers ready to attack." His gaze softened. "We can strike during their sleep cycle, limit casualties."

Beeyun sighed. His brother was right. This was bigger than himself, and obviously he'd fucked up. He hadn't realized Emma's people had started hunting him. How had he missed that? This was *his* responsibility and look how he'd botched it.

"What?" a feminine voice screeched from behind him.

He whipped around, facing his shocked lover. "Emma?"

She shook her head. "No! You can't! Just let them leave! Please, just let them leave!" Tears glistened in her eyes as she punctuated each statement with a stomp of her foot.

Beeyun stood there with his jaw dropped, everything else forgotten.

She was defending them? After they had strung her up like an animal? After they had essentially sentenced her to death. "They abused you. Don't you want to be safe from them?"

Her jaw trembled. "I am safe from them. Aren't I safe here?" She looked between him and his brother, desperation in her gaze.

"Yes, yes you are," he said, stepping forward, reaching out to comfort her, but she pulled back. Was she rejecting him?

She shook her head again, her loose hair waving about her. "I have friends there. They don't deserve this." Tears welled in her eyes, perilously close to falling now.

"Friends? Friends who sat back and watched as you were attacked by an angry mob." Any friends she had there weren't worthy of her, that much he felt certain of. He could have never stood back while a friend went through something like that.

She shook her head slowly, her voice breaking. "I told her not to. She has a family, a child. I couldn't risk them."

All the anger fled Beeyun's body. He turned helplessly to his brother, not knowing what to do, for once glad he hadn't been born first. He didn't know how anyone could make such a terrible choice.

"I can fly them," she said, stepping forward. "I can fly them home."

Beeyun flinched, some dark part of him taunting him, saying she didn't really want him, didn't want to stay with him. "No, Emma. You don't belong with them."

You belong with me.

She raised an eyebrow at him, her lips quirked into just the barest of smiles. "And I belong here?" She shook her head one last time. "No one else can do this. No one else can fly that ship. Just me."

CHAPTER FOURTEEN

---

*A*nan felt an outsider, an interloper in the conversation that followed after the little brown alien yelled out. He didn't understand every word. Clearly, his brother had learned some of her language and vice versa, but Anan could understood the basics.

The woman was upset with their plans, begged them not to. Beeyun was outraged and was that fear? Too much emotion ricocheted back and forth for the relationship to be strictly sexual. Beeyun cared, and so did the girl.

He paid close attention, listening in for the handful of words he could understand from each sentence. Anan knew when she offered a solution. He didn't understand what the solution was, though, as the critical words were from her language.

"Explain," he said, interrupting his brother's objections. "In my language, if you will. You seem to have a moderate grasp of it."

She blinked over at him, but then spoke up. "I can take them away. I'm the only one who can. They need never come back. Just don't hurt them."

Anan paused for a moment, seeing the pain etched into his brother's eyes now that they faced each other. Beeyun didn't want to be separated from the woman. Anan rocked back and forth on his heels, searching for a solution. He sighed. "They won't go quietly, will they?"

"I don't believe so, no. I don't know what's gotten into them." She stopped, her face scrunched up in concentration. Probably looking for a word. "Most of them aren't violent by nature or trade. They shouldn't have acted the way they did."

He nodded. "Maenu. We knew it had been affecting them."

"Maenu?"

"It's a plant."

Her eyes lit up. "Psychotropic."

"What?"

She shook her head. "Never mind."

"I cannot guarantee none will come to harm. In fact, I can almost guarantee some will. I will try to minimize it. Of that, you have my word. We will strike in their sleep cycle, round up all those outside the ship quietly, and you will take them away. Agreed?"

"Agreed." She looked fragile as she nodded her head.

Was she just as attached to his brother as Beeyun was to her?

Beeyun glared at him.

He needed to fix this, but how? His soldiers could attack immediately. They were ready at a moment's notice, but he hesitated. There was more at stake than just his people's safety. He peered at his brother again, who was giving him a look that said he wanted to skin him alive and leave him for carrion eaters to feast on.

"We'll reconvene once all preparations are made." He nodded and left.

I can fly them home.

Those words haunted her. Emma wanted to stay. She wanted to curl up in a ball, cling to the bed, and never leave. She thought about returning to the others and her blood ran cold, sending chills down her arms and back.

What was she thinking? She couldn't go back. They would kill her. It wasn't like she could lock herself in the control room for months. It didn't have a source of food or water.

Or a bathroom, for that matter.

Which meant she needed to risk exposing herself to the others. Were they still acting crazy? What would they do if they saw her? Would they just act cold to her as they had before landing, or would they attack her as they had right before Beeyun saved her?

Beeyun… It felt like a gaping chasm opened in her chest when she thought of him. She would never see him again. Beeyun, one of the few people who'd seen her as worthy without condition. Her parents had, but she'd never had much faith in that. They were parents. It was practically their job. But Beeyun didn't have any ulterior motives, nothing to distort his perceptions of her. He just saw *her,* and he still admired her.

In the past, every time she'd succeeded at something, it had always felt hollow, like something was missing, like it wasn't what she was looking for. Her parents had celebrated when she graduated college and again when she finished her pilot training, got her sub-space qualifications, but it had felt like she was alone in a giant room even as they encouraged her and hugged her. She'd wanted to escape, to keep searching for what was missing.

Emma hadn't felt like that once since meeting Beeyun. Even when they couldn't talk, it had been exciting, interesting. She'd looked forward to every lesson. He was a beautiful man, inside and out. He was everything she'd always dreamed of in a man, even if she'd never expected that dream man to be purple. How could she leave him?

But at the same time, how could she let Anan's army attack the other humans? None of them deserved that.

And why the hell hadn't she thought of them *once* since being rescued? She had *friends* there. Lacy, Rickelle, Jacie, they were all there. She'd left them behind and never thought about what they might be going through for even a moment. Guilt raced through her, and she pulled her arms tighter around her knees, burying her face in the bedding beside her. Eyes closed, she couldn't see the color, or how it bunched on the floor, the abandoned top sheet she'd used to entice Beeyun earlier tickling her toes.

That playful moment felt like ages ago. Emma felt gutted now, her situation overwhelming her, leaving her no room to think, to act, to plan. She needed a plan. She couldn't let them hurt Lacy and her family, but she didn't want to leave Beeyun behind either. A sob slipped out, but she locked it down before she lost control.

She needed to think.

She needed a plan.

Emma had run off to his bedroom after Anan left. Beeyun wanted to follow her, comfort her, but wasn't sure of his welcome. How could she volunteer to leave so easily? How was she okay with leaving him? Did she not feel as he did?

But then, how could she? Beeyun was nothing like her. He didn't deserve her, and he never would. He wandered through his home, but couldn't bear to stay anywhere. The kitchen was too painful, filled with both good memories and the terrible moment she'd offered to leave. He wandered down the hall. Usually, he would settle in for a bath, but even that sanctuary was tainted now, his memory filled with their encounter there.

In an absent haze, he stepped out into a beam of bright daylight that made him squint, closing his eyes as he raised his hand to block the rays. Trees surrounded him at the entrance of his home. It was so familiar, yet suddenly alien, like it had changed and he no longer recognized it.

Or was it he who had changed?

He didn't feel the same anymore. He felt broken. As he stood there, the sun warming his skin, he just felt heavy, tired. He felt like he could just sit down and never move again. Muted, the sounds of the forest drifted to him. Leaves rustled as creatures moved through the underbrush, intermixed with the occasional cry that split the air. He couldn't really connect to any of it.

What did any of it mean without Emma?

———

Hours later, Anan approached his brother's home. It was broad daylight. Streams of light filtered through the green and blue leaves. Just outside the entrance, Beeyun stood there like a statue staring out into the distance.

How long had he been standing there? As he approached, his brother looked blank, no expression on his face. The only motion was the breath entering and leaving his chest.

"Beeyun?"

He blinked, taking a moment before finally turning to Anan.

Anan felt alarmed, though he couldn't say why. Just as before, Beeyun's expression was blank, but something about it made him want to act, to do *something*. He needed to fix this. "Are you okay?" He stepped forward, hesitant to approach. Would his brother lash out at him? He'd half expected him to attack earlier when he'd mentioned organizing the troops against the aliens. He knew his brother was sensitive to any implication he couldn't do his job, but it couldn't be helped. Anan refused to risk his brother's life to save his pride.

"I'm fine," Beeyun said, his voice wooden.

Anan shook his head. "You're not."

"I'll be fine." His words that time barely reached Anan's ears.

Anan sighed. He needed to fix this. He just hoped the solution he'd come up with was the right choice. It would nearly break him. Beeyun was the only family he had. Anan tried to pull on his professional facade. It was hard with his brother before him, looking increasingly broken. "I have a task for you."

"What?" Beeyun reacted, his face slow to respond. He looked betrayed.

"I won't force you. This is not something to be entered into lightly."

Beeyun shored himself up while Anan talked. "What is it you would have of me?"

Anan paused. This was it, the point of no return. He knew what his brother's answer would be. He'd seen that when

Beeyun had reacted to the idea of her leaving and just now when he was staring off into space like a shell of himself. He would lose his brother. Anan buried his feelings as he'd done so many times since his father passed the mantle of leadership down to him. "We know nothing about what lies beyond our skies. Clearly, that is no longer wise. We must move forward. If we are to keep our people safe, we must protect ourselves from the potential dangers that loom beyond. I would like you to go with our visitors when your lady flies them away. We need to foster good relations with these long-traveling people. It may be that one day we could use such relations.

"I know this means I may not see you for some time and possibly never again. You may never be able to return home, but if you go, you go with the gratitude of your people. And the love of a brother."

"Anan, I…"

He held up a hand, silencing him. "I will miss you."

Beeyun smirked. "She might not have me."

Anan smiled. "How could she resist?"

CHAPTER FIFTEEN

nan stood off to the side. He was always separate. Central to everything, a part of nothing. It was a terrible way to live, but what choice did he have? They stood in the woods near his brother's home, waiting to send the intruders back to their planet.

Soldiers stood in organized, if noisy, groups while their commanders waited patiently for orders. Emma and Beeyun stood together, just as isolated as he was, and yet Anan couldn't help feeling proud of his brother. He was going to be a historic figure, the first of their kind to go off-world, the first of their kind to establish relations with another race. He frowned. Meanwhile, Anan would just be another in a long line of leaders, recorded in the history books, but soon forgotten.

He shifted in place, trying not to let his insecurities show. He couldn't. Everyone was counting on him. He couldn't let them down. This was the duty he'd been born to.

Anan glanced at his brother again, noticing how he seemed completely oblivious to the esteem the soldiers gave him. He always did his duty with a work ethic that would put anyone to shame, and wouldn't ever think of letting someone else take over some of his load. And yet, he never boasted, was humble almost to a fault.

I'll miss you, brother.

He needed to speak up, to start this mission, but it meant never seeing his brother again, and he had a hard time going through with it. Beeyun was the only one he could be himself around, the brother rather than the leader. What would happen to Anan once he was gone?

But as he watched his brother, he simply didn't have it in himself to be selfish. He could clearly see how Beeyun and Emma looked at each other, even when they tried to hide it. He would never wish heartache on his kin, even if it broke him.

And it wouldn't. He was a leader, strong. He would be fine. It would be different, but he would survive.

"All right, everyone. Let's get started."

Emma crouched in the trees next to Beeyun, her heart in her throat and her palms slick with sweat. Though she couldn't see them, she could *feel* the soldiers surrounding them on all sides. Anan had chosen the beginning of the next dark cycle to strike, using her own species' weakness against them. She felt bad about that, but wasn't it better than seeing someone hurt?

Then, like a wave crashing onto the shore, the soldiers moved as one. They overwhelmed the men on duty, silencing them before they could sound alarms. They threw each man over a shoulder and carried them toward the *Endeavour*.

Beeyun tightened his grip and stood, urging her to do the same. Emma took a deep breath and tried not to let her own nerves infect him. He had to be unsettled enough as it was. After all, he was leaving his people and everything he knew behind. She'd done something similar when she came here, but at least she'd still had the ship and her role as pilot to cling to. He only had her.

Well, she supposed he also had his role, but that was uncertain at best. She couldn't guarantee his safety on her ship, and he had to feel uncertain and anxious. This was new territory for his people. There was no precedent, no playbook, nothing.

I still can't believe he's coming.

Nerves settled low in her stomach. She looked up at him and wondered if there could be too much of a good thing. Would he cling too hard in the alien environment she was leading him into? But even a few moments looking up at his beautiful purple skin settled her nerves.

The meadow was cleared of all but soldiers, some of whom had much smaller human men slung over their shoulders. Beeyun tugged on her hand, pulling her across the distance at a mad dash, at least it felt that way at her much shorter stride length. They needed to lock the cockpit and get the ship off the ground before anyone knew something was amiss.

Her heart pounded as they ate up the distance, feeling desperation and guilt. The word *Betrayer* ran through her head over and over again, a not-so-subtle reminder that Beeyun, his brother, and all the soldiers around them were not her people. Would anyone understand? Would Lacy? Or would disappointment darken her friend's eyes the next time they met?

Beeyun hoisted her up by the waist when they reached the ship, dropping her on the top step where she slammed the door unlocked. It hissed open violently. The soldiers gasped, staggering back a couple steps, their grips tightening on their weapons as she looked toward them. Beeyun didn't react except to grip her waist a little tighter, his fingers pinching her sides. Emma tapped his hands and he let go, nodding to his people and stepping forward, a silent encouragement.

She turned around in the doorway, feeling unsettled. As she peered out over the men and wilds, a wave of homesickness overcame her. Emma would miss this place. She looked down at Beeyun, figuring he would want to say goodbye, but he merely nodded at his brother and ushered her inside. The flexing grip of his hands as he encouraged her forward betrayed his confidence.

A handful of the men followed them in—the ones carrying humans—and nervously shifted about, uncomfortable in the alien environment. "Put them down."

Without a second glance, she pulled Beeyun into the cockpit, locked the door with her own codes, and dropped him in the co-pilot seat. "This is necessary." She looked Beeyun in the eyes as she strapped him into the harness, unsure how he would respond to it. All he did was smile at her.

She smiled back and shook her head before throwing herself into the pilot's seat, strapping in, and kicking on the camera in the main hallway. All the security guys were on the floor unconscious, no aliens in sight. She engaged the lock on the outer doors.

"This is going to suck." No one was in their seats, none of the cargo was latched down. Somehow, she had to leave atmosphere—with all the necessary propulsion that went with it—without managing to kill anyone. What had she been thinking?

"You can do this."

Emma looked over at Beeyun, surprised by the comment. His hand touched her forearm, and he nodded his head, completely confident in her. "I have an idea," she said.

It was maybe stupid, it probably wouldn't work, and there was a possibility it would make the situation worse, but she tried it. Fiddling with the controls, she messed with the artificial gravity systems and kicked them on, hoping she could create a sort of air bag for the passengers. She'd never heard of it done before, had no idea if it would work, but at least this wasn't a MAG-GRAV system. It would have never worked on one of those.

Emma took a deep breath, programmed the exit trajectory, and hauled ass off-world. Even with the counter-measures, the inertia pulled her hard toward the back of her seat. Beside her, Beeyun gasped, and she smirked as he gave the seat arms a white-knuckled grip.

"Hold on, baby." A crazy swirl of colors passed across the SmartGlass, but the impact of takeoff lessened after that push, and Emma sighed a breath of relief. In no time, they left the planet behind them, and she slowed. Tapping at the computer, she set a course for Earth, but did not enter sub-space yet, wanting to look over at Beeyun. She worried that he might regret it. She was afraid to look. Didn't want to see regret on his face. How much would it hurt if she saw it?

"Can I… take this off now?" A hesitant and perplexed note colored his normally confident voice.

"Yes, sorry." She popped her own harness, forgetting that she'd messed with the artificial gravity systems. Her body responded in unpredictable ways to the pull from all directions. It felt like the opposite of zero gravity. Still, it had a similar effect, and she lost her grip with the floor. "Shite. Sorry." She grabbed the chair with one hand and set everything back to rights on the console with the other. "Better?"

The perplexed look hadn't left his face as she turned to him. She laughed. "I'll get you out of there in no time, big guy."

A few seconds and a couple clicks, and she had him free. She half expected him to rip the straps off, but he slipped them away calmly, studying the latches with curiosity.

"I can see where this would come in handy." He tugged on them before setting them aside. "Since this is your arena, now what?"

"Now, I need to make sure everyone is okay. We were the only two people strapped in, so some people could be hurt."

He nodded. "Is there anything I can do to help?"

"Not yet. No one else knows you're on board, and those security officers probably won't be too friendly when they wake up. I'd rather have you here, behind a locked door, until I know that everyone will accept you. There aren't a lot of places to run or hide on a ship like this. You're big and strong, but humans are pack creatures. We don't fight fair and generally prefer fighting in groups."

He nodded. "There's nothing I can do here?"

She patted his arm. "Not at the moment. That would require a lot of teaching, which I don't have time for right this second. I need to check that everyone is okay and make sure the systems are in good repair."

He nodded again, but Emma didn't know if he really understood all she'd said. They'd come a long way, but he had no frame of reference for any of this. Even his impressive skills with learning language wouldn't help if he didn't understand what the item itself was.

"Don't worry. This is just temporary."

He nodded and settled back in his seat.

"Emma?"

Emma froze, shifting her gaze toward the voice.

We're not alone.

Lacy had been at the bunks trying to get her daughter to sleep when it happened.

The door to the control room had unlocked with a click, and she froze, putting herself bodily between the door and her loved ones. She'd turned, ready to face whomever had circumvented the room's security. For a moment, she'd thought she was dreaming.

Emma's back.

It had seemed impossible… and perfect. She'd almost cried, then another barreled into the room behind her friend and she froze once more. He was big, purple, and looked a little shellshocked. Lacy latched onto the frame of the top bunk to ground herself, the cool metal digging into her palm.

What's going on?

She couldn't form words, couldn't believe her eyes. Sure, she'd suspected an alien might have taken Emma, hoped even. After all, a sentient being might look after her. An animal would probably just eat her. More than anything, she'd wanted to believe her friend was okay, that protecting her family hadn't meant Emma's death.

But Emma was alive and bringing an alien aboard their ship. Why? What was going on?

Then everything changed. The engines came to life, and it felt like she was being pulled in all directions at once. *What the hell's going on?* She clung even harder to the bed frame and looked back at her wife and daughter. Jacie was sitting up, watching the goings on with wide eyes.

Then the ship took off. Lacy sucked in a gasp that strangled in her throat as the ship slammed her into the wall behind her.

Jacie. Rick.

Were they okay? None of them were strapped in. They could have hit their heads during takeoff. She wanted to look, check, but until they escaped gravity, it would be impossible. She could barely move.

Moments passed, and she let out a long breath as they slowed and everything returned to normal. She immediately turned, touching first Jacie then Rick. Jacie was fussy, having little patience with her. She was fine. Rickelle smiled at her affectionately, then her own eyes rounded as she looked over Lacy's head.

She's spotted the alien, too.

Lacy turned, and Rick's hand dropped onto her shoulder in support. Her heart pounded in her chest as she took in the situation. Emma was messing with the alien's harness, talking to him, but Lacy felt like she was underwater, the words washing over her, muffled and unintelligible.

"Emma?" Her voice trembled as she finally got a word out.

Emma jerked and turned slowly in Lacy's direction, looking wary.

Why is she wary of me?

"What's going on?"

Emma released a slow breath. "I can explain."

***

A tiny ball of fur shook its head, a little dazed from the sudden jarring when the ground itself moved beneath it. It got to its feet, its joints bent to better prepare for the ground to move again, but nothing happened. The ground did seem a little unsteady, and it pressed itself low, but the loud roar was gone, nothing but a gentle hum remaining. It chuffed, shaking its head again, and got back to its feet.

It sniffed the air, searching for predators, but smelled nothing but an unfamiliar, cold tang. Not liking the scent, it shook its head again, trying to rid itself of the offensive odor. Next, it blinked, shifting the nictitating lens over its eyes. The world turned from an ugly gray, which made it nervous, to a brilliant world of reds, oranges, blues, and whites.

It moved toward a patch of white, hungry.

CHAPTER SIXTEEN

While everything else was cold, unpleasant, and even alarming, Beeyun was captured by the view. He'd never seen his home from above before, and the beauty of it took his breath away.

Shocked by the force of the beast they rode in, he almost didn't look in time. He'd been so focused on holding on for dear life, he'd almost missed it, which would have been a shame. To think, not one of his kind had seen this before. It made him think Emma's people didn't have it all wrong after all.

But the view when the beast calmed down? Incomparable. A sphere hovered below them in a swirl of colors unlike anything he'd ever seen in his life. He could see the great ocean, and when they'd been lower, he'd made out the cross-shaped mountain range that had brought his people together again. Beyond the planet, the stars winked at him in a way he'd never seen before, bright pinpoints of light in a sea of black so intense chills ran down his spine.

Emma worked at his side, trying to reassure him, even if he was completely useless in this environment. But that didn't stop him from eating up the sight of Emma in her natural role. Her hands glided over the many surfaces, seemingly controlling this massive beast with the very tips of her fingers. He didn't understand it, but he did sit back in awe as he watched.

Images popped up on the window overlooking the stars, showing what he assumed were other rooms in this great beast. Ship, she'd called it. Her gaze scanned each image, then her fingers flew over her controls again, pulling up another.

He wanted to ask questions, but he feared if he asked one, they would all spill out like a flood, drowning them both. Beeyun wanted to know everything. Unfortunately, he couldn't absorb this as he could language. He would have to learn the hard way. Though, learning the hard way from Emma had ample appeal.

A loud banging rattled the door behind them. Beeyun spun in his chair, glaring at it, tensed for a fight. "Would you like me to handle this?" he asked, eyes narrowed.

She sighed and shook her head. "No, no need." Leaning forward, she tapped something. Beeyun shifted to see what she'd done, but her hand moved too fast to see. "Hello? How can I help you?" she said in a deceptively cheery tone, a smirk on her face.

"What the hell, Emma?!" a man yelled, his voice projecting into the room. The volume distorted his words. He banged on the door a couple more times for good measure. "Why did we take off?"

"No choice, Captain."

The door rattled again. "And why in hell is this door locked?"

She shrugged, even though the disembodied voice couldn't see her.

"What is he grumbling about?" the other female said, Emma's friend. "We've kept that door locked since you were rescued." She looked at Beeyun with a mixture of gratitude and wariness.

He could accept that. She had no reason to trust him yet. He smiled at her, hoping it came across as reassuring.

Emma touched something, rolling her eyes in Beeyun's direction. "No offense, sir, but people weren't exactly kind to me last time. I didn't want to take any chances."

Beeyun flinched at the reminder of how they'd come together, his hands balling into fists, his nails biting into his palms painfully.

Shuffling noises came through along with the voice. "Yeah, I don't know what that was. I'm sorry."

"Yeah, well, I do. That's why we had to leave." Then she muttered under her breath, "Among other things."

"What was that?"

"Nothing, Captain."

Beeyun smirked, then pointed to himself in question.

She shook her head. "Again, no offense, but I'd rather keep the door locked until I'm confident of my safety, sir."

A sigh came across, then the sound cut out entirely.

"What was that?" Beeyun leaned forward, looking back where she'd pressed on the panel.

"This," she pointed, "is a comm. There's three buttons. This is what we just used, and it connects to the spot right outside the door. This one is ship-wide so anyone can hear. And this will broadcast out to anything with a compatible system."

He nodded. "It allows you to speak to those you cannot see or hear normally?"

"Bingo." She pointed a finger at him and smiled.

"Bingo?" He hadn't heard that word before.

"Affirmative? Correct?"

He nodded. "Understood."

She reached out and gripped his hand real quick before getting back to work.

"What are you doing now?" He leaned farther forward, hoping she would not only tell him what she was doing but how.

"I'm going to take the ship into sub-space."

"Sub-space?"

She turned and looked at him, wringing her hands. "Well, the distance between my home and yours is so great, under ordinary circumstances, we could never reach it in a lifetime."

Beeyun blanched, wondering what he'd gotten himself into. Sure, his brother had said he might never return home, but he'd held the idea in the back of his head as a possibility, not an inevitability. His gut twisted at never going home again, never seeing his family, but the thought of never seeing Emma again nearly made him physically ill, so he shook his head. Whatever happened, he was where he needed to be. He would miss his family. He didn't know if he would want to live with missing Emma.

"Sub-space allows us to arrive in a fraction of the time. It'll still take months. Um, a month would be about ten of your days? Anyway, sub-space itself is more compact. The distance between things is smaller. And some distances aren't proportional. It's not the easiest thing to navigate, and maps are hard to rely on. It's easy to get caught in the gravity of planets and such.

"Still, we could have never made the trip otherwise. And no matter how it ended up, I'm glad we did." She smiled, the smile lighting up her face and lightening his heart.

"So how do we do this, then?"

Beeyun watched and listened, trying to learn and absorb everything he could, even when he knew he was missing large segments of foundational information he had no hope of getting at the moment. He would learn. Emma would teach him.

And as they jumped into sub-space, his jaw dropped. If he'd thought his home striking from above, sub-space set a whole new standard. Emma hadn't lied when she said distances were compressed and inconsistent. Great spherical bodies that had seemed little more than dots before loomed close, alarming him at their proximity, but Emma traversed the empty terrain as if made for it.

They cruised through at a steady pace, though he couldn't fathom how fast they were traveling as he'd lost all perception of scale long before this. As time passed, his grip on his seat slackened, and he started to relax, getting acclimated to the strange, unwelcoming environment. He couldn't imagine anyone being comfortable in such a cold place.

"It's not as bad as all that."

"What?" He jerked in his seat, looking over at Emma.

"You're right that it's cold."

He'd spoken aloud?

"And there is nothing like getting out once the journey's over. Even though you can get up and walk around, you get stir crazy, and the natural world has a tendency of setting your soul at peace. But then, so does this view." Beeyun looked out the window again. They passed what reminded him of brightly colored clouds, fluffy and fuzzy on the edges, but distinct enough to identify. It felt like an artist's imagination, colorful and stylized.

He couldn't help but agree with Emma's assessment. Beeyun had a hard time imagining spending months here, but the thrill of learning, exploring, and being with Emma made up for it.

Besides, a few months was nothing.

* * *

Lacy was quiet at the back of the room. At first, she held Jacie back, clutching her like a safety blanket, but Rick had climbed down from the top bunk, nudging her arm and giving her that look, the one that said she was smothering their daughter again.

She'd sighed and released her. Jacie had immediately made a beeline for the alien. Beeyun, Emma had called him.

He looks so human.

Rick wrapped an arm around her, pulling her into her side. She rested her head on her shoulder as Jacie tugged on Beeyun's sleeve, asking him question after question. He talked slowly, with the occasional word she didn't understand interspersed with English. How did he know English? It hadn't been that long since he stole Emma away. It seemed impossible that his grasp of their language could be so good after so short a time. Still, her daughter's constant questions as she bounced against the arm of the alien's chair were surprisingly familiar. She almost relaxed until another bang crashed into the door, jerking her out of her calm.

"Easy," Rick said into her ear.

Beeyun controlled the comm this time, letting Emma focus on flying. He didn't speak though, looking to Emma for guidance.

"What the fuck?" a man's voice said.

She flinched, her hands flexing, wanting to cover her daughter's ears.

"Can I help you?" Emma said, sounding exasperated.

"You can tell me who the fuck attacked us! Were you involved in this? I bet you were, you little shit."

Lacy pushed out of her wife's arms and strode across the room, looking at Emma as she reached the control panel. "How do I mute?"

"That button," Emma said, pointing as she kept one hand on the controls.

"I'm ending this conversation," she said before hitting the mute button.

The banging continued, but they could no longer hear the bastard's voice.

The room was otherwise eerily quiet.

CHAPTER SEVENTEEN

Captain West stood in the mess hall, ready to address the crew and passengers. It hadn't even been a day since they took off, but already, unrest was sowing its way through the ranks. As he scanned the room, he marveled over the lack of any serious injuries. The security crew had bumps on their heads from being attacked, but otherwise only a few bumps and bruises marred his people, raising the pilot in his esteem a little. He'd never given her a lot of credit, and she certainly deserved more after that impressive display of piloting.

Instead, he'd always given her a hard time. But in spite of everything, she'd only ever tried to help, often working harder and at more varied tasks than anyone else. And what did she get for all her efforts? Strung up like a piece of meat. He shook his head, still not believing how low they'd gotten before all their heads seemed to clear.

"Ahem!" He cleared his throat, reaching out one hand to the ceiling to get everyone's attention. Not that it worked.

The security crew stood off to the side, arms crossed in front of them, vibrating with rage. A couple had faces red with anger, and some kept trying to rile up the others, which worked more often than not, sending a wave of agitation and aggression through the room.

"People, people, calm down!" West's voice boomed, causing a moment of silence before it started up again.

Everyone seemed to take affront at the idea of calming down. If anything, that eye of a storm just served as contrast for how much worse it could get. Shouts about "backstabbing purple fuckers" came from his left, along with "betraying bitch," which he assumed referred to the pilot. In front of him, selfish sentiments echoed through the room, a whole lot of questions like "But what about us?" and "What about our equipment?" and "What about our research?" One clear voice shouted, "I'm not ready to turn back home. Turn this damn ship around!"

West opened his mouth, wanting to give them details, tell them why they couldn't, but he didn't have them. Emma had been vague over the intercom, only saying their aggressive behavior had been the reason they'd had to leave, whatever that meant. He needed to talk to her again, and in the meantime, utter anarchy reigned around him.

God, he'd thought things were getting better.

"Everyone, everyone, please," a gentle voice called into the room, ironically powerful in the chaotic din.

West stared at the woman, trying to place her as the room settled down a little. She continued speaking, the tone of her voice alone continuing its spell on the group.

His eyes widened in recognition. The pilot's friend. He couldn't remember her name, but he did remember her and her family locking themselves in the control room, afraid of their out-of-control group. Bile rose in his throat at what could have happened to that little family with how insane they'd all become.

Or any of the families, for that matter. Everyone with children had become scarce of late. Would they have stopped at hurting a child? He wasn't sure. Hell, he still couldn't believe what they'd done to that woman. Logic and all sense had completely flown from their heads, and it still shocked him. After all, they could have been stuck on that planet permanently if they'd lost her. What the hell had been wrong with them?

He intended to ask Emma. He suspected she knew.

After another five or ten minutes, the woman's soft voice backed by his stern presence seemed to settle peace over them once more, and the group disbanded, though unsettled waters still traveled close to the surface.

When the last of them left, West turned to her and reached out a hand. "Thanks for your help there. I don't know what I would have done if you hadn't stepped in." He shook his head. "This entire mission has been FUBAR from the very beginning."

She smiled. "Yeah, and the only one who seemed to really see it was Emma."

"Really?"

She nodded. "She was always pointing out things that were off, annoying you with her suggestions, staring off into the tree line. Before you guys attacked her, she told us to run. She told me to grab my family and get in the ship."

West's jaw dropped.

"I don't think she knew exactly what was going to happen, but I know she didn't want my daughter to see, and she didn't want me caught in the crossfire. Even once she was tied up, she still told me to go." She didn't look at West then, staring off into space.

"I'm sorry."

A desolate look settled over her face as she looked up at him. "You should be." She turned to leave.

"Wait. I didn't catch your name."

She turned again, looking almost disgusted. "Lacy."

The quiet echoed off the walls in her absence. No one on the ship was worth being around in that moment, not even him.

Emma slowed the ship down, then stopped somewhere safe. Checking the coordinates for even the slightest fluctuations, she sat back with a sigh when nothing budged. "That's it for the day."

Beeyun glanced out through the SmartGlass, then back at her. "That's it? We don't keep going?"

She looked over at him. "Some missions, yeah. This one, no. There's only one pilot, and you can't run autopilot in sub-space. Our species has invented a lot of amazing things, but we still haven't come up with an autopilot that can handle the challenges of flying out here. Heck, most pilots aren't even rated for sub-space."

"How many are?"

Emma frowned. "Maybe… twenty or twenty-five percent?"

"That doesn't sound like much."

"It's not."

"Why only one pilot?"

"Not enough funding? Not enough support? I don't quite know how to explain it properly. I mean, I'd only be guessing, anyway."

Beeyun turned his gaze back to the control panels, his hands fluttering.

"Here. Let me show you a few things you can do tomorrow to help." She pointed out how to monitor the displays, explaining the min and max readings for each. Some displays she didn't explain, but he could help by watching them and reporting to her. It would allow her to focus more on the flying and less on the ship.

The door lock behind them disengaged. Emma turned and smiled as Lacy stepped through. Lacy zeroed in on Emma for a hug that nearly crushed her lungs.

"What are you, a bodybuilder?"

Lacy laughed, pulling away. "No, just grateful to see a friend after that nightmare of a meeting. People here are nuts."

Beeyun pressed a button out of the corner of her eye and the lock on the door engaged with a reassuring click. She hadn't even taught him that one yet.

Emma needed to use the bathroom and get her and Beeyun some food, but she kept putting it off, hesitant to enter the hallway. The control room represented safety for her. And she knew full well how the others felt about her. She was unwanted.

Betrayer.

Bitch.

At least, she had Beeyun, Lacy, and her family. Though, now that the day was over, she realized they had to figure out sleeping arrangements. She turned to her friend.

What do we do now?

CHAPTER EIGHTEEN

Beeyun sat off to the side as Emma embraced and joked with her friend.

"How's your family?" Emma smiled, causing his heart to stutter at the sight. Her smiles had been rare since she'd announced she could take her people away. A part of him still expected her to be relieved at coming back, but she'd rarely left this room. Each time she did, anxiety rushed through him. He remembered how her people had treated her, how he'd had to save her.

She never wanted to come back.

No, she didn't return because she wanted to. She returned to protect her people, protect them in a way he wished he'd been able to do. It was his brother who'd sent them packing, his brother who had given him this new role, a role he wasn't remotely qualified for. Their people hadn't needed such a role since the four tribes reunited generations ago.

He glanced to the cold, metal door, a uniform gray that left him a little grateful that Emma had refused to let him roam the ship. It was all too much, too new. He felt insecure at the best of times, but this place? With no understanding of the technology? Feeling completely out of sorts? Nothing was familiar to him here except Emma, and even she was an alien.

"Good enough now," Lacy said, leaning against the nearest smooth surface and jarring him from his thoughts. "It was rough going for a while there. Not that I have to tell you that." She looked over at him for a split second before returning to the conversation. "We spent more than a little time locked in this room." She shook her head. "Everyone went nuts."

He frowned. The woman spoke quickly, and while he could understand many of the words she used, a lot of the meaning eluded him. He looked to Emma, hoping for something, assurances or a translation maybe, but she hung on every word the other woman said, not even noticing him. Emotion boiled in his gut, but he pushed it down, not willing to give it audience.

Lacy waved her hand in front of her face, like swatting a bug, yet another thing he didn't understand. "Never mind that, though. I want to know what happened to you." She looked over at Beeyun again meaningfully. "Last I knew, a purple streak was running away with you. I'm assuming that would be this big guy."

Emma looked over at him and smiled, and for a moment, he forgot how lost and alone he felt in the room with her friend. "Yeah, that was him. He saved me and we've been learning to communicate ever since."

Lacy turned back to him again. "I hate to ask, but how did you rip those buildings apart?"

He gave her a wicked smile and waved his fingers in front of himself.

Emma laughed, wrapping her arms around her torso. Lacy just looked between them as if they'd lost their ever-loving minds. Emma sucked in a breath and shook her head, still smiling.

"I feel like I just stepped in the middle of a joke I have no hope of getting."

"Beeyun has retractable claws."

Lacy whipped her head around, focusing on his fingertips as if she feared he would lash out at her.

He wanted to reassure her, but all his communications with Emma thus far had been a combination of her language and his own. In the end, he settled on a single word. "Safe." He looked into her eyes and hoped what she saw there portrayed his intent.

Emma yawned, and her friend turned away.

"I should let you guys get some sleep. It's been a long day." She pushed up from her perch, walking past Beeyun before leaning in, her hand resting gently on his shoulder, and whispering, "Thank you."

"Wait, Lacy. Where are you staying?" Emma said, jumping up from her perch.

Lacy shook her head. "Just back to the rooms we had before. I think it should be safe, now. Things are still tense, but it feels like people are, for the most part, sane again." She frowned. "But I'd be careful, Emma. There are still some people who don't look on you kindly. That meeting was not pretty today." Without a backward glance, she ushered her family from the room and left them to their solitude.

Silence reigned for a spell as Emma stood to prepare for sleep, leaving Beeyun to his thoughts.

Yet again, he'd met someone who made him think he'd seriously misjudged their species. Her words of thanks had floored him. How could she be so accepting of someone who had actively worked at sabotaging them for days? He'd only met a handful of them, but all of them proved to be generous and honorable. Or sweet. He smiled. The little girl, Jacie, was adorable.

He turned to watch Emma get ready for bed. Mayhap the maenu had more impact on their species than he'd thought. Had he been too hasty to judge them? Perhaps if he'd tried communicating with them first, there could have been a different outcome.

Emma settled into her small bunk while Beeyun continued to stare absently out the SmartGlass. She smiled, remembering the horror on his face when she'd pointed out the sleeping arrangements. There were two bunks, neither of which seemed long enough for his tall frame.

By the time Lacy had left, it was growing late. While here, Lacy had brought food to them so Emma only had to leave the control room to use the bathroom, but it occurred to her that Beeyun hadn't left once.

Before bringing him to the bathrooms, she'd checked all the halls, determined not to put him at risk. He was her responsibility, and she couldn't bear him being hurt. When the coast was clear, she'd led him to the nearest bathroom, and they'd both handled their business before locking up the control room once more.

Emma had changed, curled up in bed, and watched him as he sat staring out at the stars, her thoughts drifting.

Why did I do this?

She'd never wanted to return. She could admit that to herself. While she would have missed Lacy, there was no downside to staying with Beeyun. She'd liked his home, felt welcome, and even his odd brother had made her feel accepted, even if she sometimes didn't understand his motives.

Heat rose to her cheeks, remembering him catching them in the act. She shook her head against her pillow. Hell, even with that unendingly embarrassing encounter, she still would have taken that over returning. Back now, she was reminded all over again that she wasn't wanted. Countless times throughout the day, people had banged on the door, demanding an explanation, even cursing her very existence. No, she hadn't needed Lacy to remind her that people weren't happy with her. She *knew* they didn't want her here, *knew* she would never fit in.

And she suspected once they knew about Beeyun, it would only get worse. Right now, some of them might *think* she'd conspired with aliens against them, but there would be no doubt once they discovered him on board.

Really, Lacy was the only saving grace. She and her family had accepted Emma from the very start. She'd never once felt judged or like an outsider with them.

Emma watched him as her eyes grew heavy, wishing the bunks could fit two, already missing cuddling up to him back in the cave, his heat settling into her bones. She felt cold and alone, disconnected. She sighed, and he turned around. Tensing in his seat, he looked ready to come to her. She hadn't meant to disturb him. Shooing him off with her hand, she rolled over, facing the wall. She would never get any sleep if she stared at him all night.

With another yawn, she let sleep take her, a single thought drifting through her head.

I wonder what he'll think of Earth.

Slam.

Loud cursing, more understandable from the tone rather than the words themselves, and the sound of flesh impacting metal jarred Emma awake.

Thud.

Another curse, followed by a groan.

Emma opened her eyes and looked over the edge of her bunk at the floor, where Beeyun lay half dazed.

"Are you okay?" She looked him over, searching for signs of injury, but the room was dark, with only the dimmest light allowing her to see the contours of his face outlined in shadow. His white shirt gleamed in the darkness, making it hard to make out anything else.

He stared up at her, and the look said it all. *Are you nuts?*

Yup, not okay.

"I don't know how you can sleep on that thing. It's sized for a child. It's so short I must curl up to get on it, which causes me to hang off the sides. And it's so close to the ceiling that I can barely move without hitting something." He glared at the offending furniture for good measure.

An exhausted smile crossed her face, and she glanced to the bunk in question. Even at her much smaller stature, she had trouble with the clearance. Now that she really thought about it, the idea of Beeyun even *trying* to get on that bed sounded like something out of an SNL skit.

With a groan, she stood, using Beeyun's bunk to keep her upright as her half-brain-dead body tried to function. She stared at the fastenings for the mattress for several long minutes before her brain caught up and told her how to undo them. Then, with clumsy fingers, she separated the mattress from the bunk and dumped it on the floor on top of Beeyun.

She didn't have the energy to be gentle.

Next she collapsed to her knees and repeated the process with her own mattress. It went a little faster as her brain started to wake up. Unfortunately, she'd mostly woken by the time she lined the two small mattresses together on the floor, tossing blankets and pillows on top.

"This is better anyway," she mumbled as she snuggled under the covers and tried to fall back asleep.

"Thank you," Beeyun said, wrapping his arms around her, and suddenly sleep welcomed her.

CHAPTER NINETEEN

aptain West had a powder keg on his hands. And he didn't know how to fix it. He was a captain, for crying out loud! This wasn't in the job description. He'd hoped yesterday's meeting would help, but it hadn't. And ordinarily, he would call in Security to handle any skirmishes, but his Security personnel seemed to be the worst culprits. He slammed a body into the nearest wall, using his surroundings to his advantage since his opponents outnumbered him.

His taser took down two of them before a swift blur knocked it out of his hand, sending the device careening down the hallway until it hit the wall with a loud cracking noise. He didn't hold high hopes that it had survived the fight intact. West just hoped *he* survived the fight intact.

A man yelped as West yanked his arm tight behind his back, then used him as a shield as another came racing at him with violence bordering on madness in his eyes. West's heart raced in his throat as the barely audible snap of breaking bones drifted to his ears.

That could have been me.

Dropping the dead weight, the half conscious man groaned as he left him behind. West faced his final opponent. "See reason." He tried. He had to try, but he knew it wouldn't do any good. Lacy wasn't here this time, and clearly he wasn't cut out to be a peacekeeper.

His opponent swung, his motions quick as a snake, too quick for West's skills. Pain seared his senses in a white-hot supernova starting at his jaw and obliterating everything else.

Stay standing.

He staggered for one terrifying moment, his mind incapable of processing his surroundings. He swayed to the left.

Where is he?

His mind still hadn't caught up with the present, but he kept moving, knowing a moving target would be much less likely to get hit.

His vision cleared, the pain in his jaw down to an insistent throb. "Just back off, damn it!" Another swing, and thank Christ, he managed to dodge this one. He fisted a set of handcuffs in his palm, figuring either he could cuff him or use it like a set of brass knuckles. At this point, either option seemed good to him.

***

Emma woke up in Beeyun's arms, his reassuring warmth and weight causing her to wiggle closer. She closed her eyes again and relished the moment of peace first thing in the morning. All was quiet, and she felt relaxed, boneless even. She didn't want to get up.

It didn't last long.

Eyes closed, an insistent flashing light behind her eyelids tweaked her out of her moment. She opened them again and turned a glare toward the console. An insistent red light waited impatiently. With some careful maneuvering, she managed to get out of bed without waking Beeyun, then slinked over to the console.

"Damage alert," she muttered under her breath. With a flurry of her fingers over the controls, she pulled up the damage report. "A short in a sensor array. Cargo level."

She looked back at Beeyun, then at the currently locked door. Her mind flashed to that terrible moment when everyone turned on her. The phantom feel of wire digging into skin sent chills down her spine, but she shook the feeling away. "It's done. Past."

But the past can still hurt you.

She really should check out that short, but she didn't trust she would be safe with her crew, and as her gaze drifted back to Beeyun, her guts twisted up. He definitely would *not* be safe. And while last night, it had been quiet, no one in the halls, now it was morning. They'd slept late and the halls would have plenty of people in them. It was unlikely she could check on the short unscathed.

Emma looked back, tapping the console absently as she stared at that blinking red light.

West readjusted his jacket as he approached the control room once more. Would this meeting go better than any of the rest lately? He'd managed to secure the violent offenders, though he'd had to get creative since the *Endeavour* didn't have jails cells or any equivalent. That, and the few lockable rooms had to be locked from the control room.

His hand hesitated as it hovered in front of the control room door, his knuckles scraping the smooth surface. A sick feeling settled in his gut. He and every person on board this craft were subject to the whims and mercies of the woman on the other side of this door. He'd never felt it more than in this moment. He felt as if he'd never truly had any control at all. How had he so thoroughly taken her for granted?

Getting over himself, he knocked twice, conscious of how firmly he rapped, not wanting to come off as aggressive. There had been entirely too much aggression of late.

"Who is it?" Emma's lilting British accent called over the speaker panel near the door.

"West." He decided to try a different approach this time. No titles, no hierarchy. Just two people trying to get everyone back home in one piece.

She sighed, and another mumbled voice drifted in the background. "What do you want, West?"

"I have the worst culprits locked down in the cargo hold. I would prefer to lock them in rooms instead of chaining them together like chattel, but I had to make do since the control room was off limits."

The speaker cut off. Had he lost her? Did she believe him?

Damn it, had that come across as aggressive? Maybe he shouldn't have made the comment about the control room being off limits. Was his tone wrong? Damn, he'd never second guessed himself so much in his entire life.

"Who are you using for security?"

West laughed, the sound void of any humor. "Me."

An oddly toned, snorted laugh came through, too low in pitch to be the pilot's voice. Someone else was in that room. The only people Emma seemed to trust were Lacy and her family, and he'd spotted them in the mess hall on his way to the control room.

Besides, none of them had voices that low either.

It came to him like a strike of lightning, so simple and yet electrifying, charging his system and demanding a response.

"You brought an alien onto my ship!" His entire body stiffened in outrage, forgetting all about his promise to keep this meeting amicable.

"Beeyun," the deep voice said.

West paused, shaking out his arms, not wanting to be rash. He'd been entirely too rash entirely too often on this trip. He couldn't afford it anymore. Hell, he couldn't afford it before, but he'd also lost all sense. He took a deep breath. "We haven't been properly introduced. I'm Captain West, and I'm responsible for this ship and the people on board."

A grunt sounded, then the speaker cut off again. He couldn't help feeling like a negotiator attempting to talk down a hostage taker, which was a surprisingly apt analogy.

An alien? On board the *Endeavour*? He wanted to believe that it wouldn't be a problem, that their two peoples could co-exist, but he knew differently. The people on board this ship had been through too much strife. The wounds were too raw, too fresh. He didn't know if any of them would be tolerant enough to not attack on sight.

It would probably help if everyone knew what the hell had happened, why they'd been shipped off-world. Those without wounded egos from having their asses handed to them were upset because their stay was cut short, a project years in the making scrapped. He knew for some of the scientists, the loss was crushing.

The speaker kicked on again. "Sorry about that, Captain."

"It's quite all right. I was coming here to tell you that you should be safe outside the control room. I'm not sure if your friend, Beeyun, would be though. You know how volatile humans can be. I just can't predict how they'll react right now."

Someone grunted. Beeyun, from the depth of it.

"Yeah, humans are predictably unpredictable," Emma said.

"I do believe we could calm the situation more if we explained why the mission had to be scrapped." And not having that information might explain why the meeting yesterday had gone to shit. Then again, he also suspected no one had been ready to listen to reason, either.

"Probably, but if we put everyone in one room, it won't be pretty," Emma said.

West winced, feeling like an idiot. *That's exactly what I did. Why didn't I listen to her before now?* Could he have avoided that mess if he'd just split the meeting into a bunch of smaller ones? In his mind, he saw how they fed off each other, each outburst fueling the next. Yes, he should have done things differently. "What do you suggest?" he said with a sigh.

"Split the sessions into small groups, no more than five, I'd say. It encourages people to think individually, makes the crowd easier to manage, and reduces the chances of an instigator inciting a mob."

He flinched again. If it hadn't been for Lacey, he *would* have had a mob on his hands. "I can do that. And Emma?"

"Yeah?"

"Leave Beeyun behind. You can mention he's aboard, but let's get everyone accustomed to the idea before they meet him."

Emma shut down the comm when all she could hear was West's boots pounding on the floor.

"They were reasonable requests," Beeyun said, still staring at the speaker as he would a person.

"I think that's the most reasonable I've ever heard him be."

Beeyun nodded, moving away from the wall. "Yes, his previous conversation had a much different tone."

Emma smirked. She'd noticed that his English seemed to smooth out rapidly, using less of his native tongue each day. There was even a noticeable difference since returning to the ship, which hadn't even been two days yet.

"How do you do that?" She'd been doing her best to learn his language and felt she'd been doing a pretty good job, but she had nothing on him. His brain seemed like a computer, cataloging and adding to his knowledge at lightning speed, picking words up after being used once, extrapolating from what had already been said.

"How do I do what?"

"Learn language so fast."

He smiled, the warmth in his eyes making her forget her question.

He pointed near his ear. "I have a language chip. There are actually five languages on my world. I have only used one of them with you, the one used universally. The others are rarely spoken anymore and fed into the universal one, which came much later. This chip allowed us to understand one another when the continent reunited us."

"Reunited?"

He nodded, sitting down in the co-pilot's chair. "Many thousands of years ago, when our people lived much simpler lives…"

Emma snorted, and he glared at her. "Please continue." She covered her mouth.

"We lived on four continents. They were separated by great waterways that could only be crossed by the Tannar."

"Tannar?"

"Great flying beasts, the largest beasts on our planet. A great drought occurred, which eventually killed off the Tannars' primary food source, causing it to become extinct as well. As time passed, we forgot about each other and evolved four separate languages.

"Then the lands moved beneath us, creating the great mountain ranges and reuniting our four peoples. Except we could not talk with each other anymore. We created the chips to collect information about the four languages so we could one day communicate. The chips were later programmed to also translate language instead of just collecting it."

"And that's how you're learning English?"

He nodded. "If I were back home, I could upload the information so all my people could download it."

Emma frowned. "Then where did the fifth language come from?"

He smirked. "Politics. I suppose we could have continued on with the four languages, but when we consolidated into a single leadership instead of four tribes, it became a topic of contention. We were all equals, of course, so no one could decide what language we should speak once we could understand each other. Each tribe felt their language was superior, and they argued ceaselessly over it. Eventually, it was decided they would create a new language, easy to learn, and using equal parts from each tribe's vocabulary. If a word or concept was too important across all tribes, they would create a new one."

"Basically, a bunch of spoiled children who didn't know how to share?"

Beeyun laughed. "Yes, I suppose that could be a fitting description. In a way, the creation of a new language was central to forming a single, consolidated nation of the Danaus. It was a peace agreement, showing each tribe as equal and that each had its own strengths and characteristics to bring to the whole."

"That's kind of nice." If only humans could figure something like that out. Thinking of humans drew Emma's mind back to the conversation with the captain. "Are you okay with that? With waiting here until I've talked with the crew?" She worried about him. She felt like she was leaving a puppy behind to go to work, which was a terrible way to think of a sentient being.

Beeyun frowned. "I don't like it, but I can see the logic in the suggestion."

"I should be safe." *So will you.*

"I won't be able to protect you."

No, but I can protect you.

CHAPTER TWENTY

*B*eeyun sat impatiently in the control room. He didn't like it. Every instinct in his body told him to be out *there* protecting her. But they had a point, her and that West. A "Catch-22" as Emma had called it once. He wished to protect her from the unstable aliens, but if he went out there now, it would likely negate her very purpose in making these little sessions.

He followed Emma's instructions, and a view of Emma sitting in a room came to life in front of him. Beeyun didn't completely understand the technology, or how an image of her could be right beside that of the stars around them. He had a tablet, so it wasn't completely alien to him. But he'd spent so much time at home, away from the heart of his people's technological advancement, that even these small things weren't similar enough to make him comfortable.

His heart calmed in his chest as he watched her smiling and chatting with the woman she'd let into the control room earlier, the one who'd been there when they first arrived. In the periphery, he caught glimpses of a male, West, he guessed.

Nothing is going to happen. He tried to reassure himself, but all he wanted was for Emma to return to the safety of the control room. Why did his brother choose him for this? He didn't have the patience to be diplomatic. At least, not where she was involved.

He wanted to protect her and not just physically. Beeyun could already see the toll being here was taking on her. He wanted to wrap her up in his arms and give her a reason to feel safe and secure. He wanted her to feel important, like she mattered. She was strong, stronger than him where it mattered, and he wanted her to see that.

He needed to *make* her see that.

Emma leaned back in her seat as West led a small group of people into the mess hall. Lacy smiled at everyone reassuringly, but mostly they just glared at Emma, as if all their problems lay with her. Like with most every previous session, people hesitated, standing next to the chairs, as if having a height advantage soothed their bruised egos.

"Please sit." Emma reached out a hand.

Some crept around, never taking their eyes off her, as if sizing up a predator. She resisted the urge to roll her eyes. Two others stood behind their chairs, white-knuckled grips on the backs and jaws clenched.

"I know you all have your questions. This mission didn't go as we anticipated, and some of you are angry about that." Emma glanced away, not wanted to see how they felt about her.

"Didn't go as anticipated?" One of them released the grip on his seat back and took an aggressive step forward.

West peeled away from the wall.

Emma shook her head. "Yes. We went into this mission without sufficient information, and it bit us in the ass."

"What are you talking about?" a seated woman on her left said, leaning forward. She had scientist written all over her, a curious glimmer in her eye.

"Well, first, as you may have guessed, the planet was not unoccupied. It is the seat of a fairly advanced civilization. Some technologies we have, they don't. Like vehicles. They have native species that have made developing more advanced modes of travel superfluous. But they also have technologies that make it clear they are quite advanced, like solar-powered tablets and advanced translation implants. Their technology made it so that within a matter of days, he'd started to learn English words, even grammar structure."

The man who'd spoken earlier scoffed. "Yeah, right. Did you see those structures? The damage? That wasn't the work of an intelligent species. It was a monster."

"Really? We set up shop in his backyard. Don't we have castle doctrine laws back on Earth? A person is allowed to defend their home."

He turned to the others. "Do you believe this shit? This traitor," he spat the word at her, "is trying to make us believe she ruined years of our work over some, what, tribal monsters and their so-called technology?"

"Monsters? Really? What about his actions sound like a monster? He waited until everyone was asleep before sabotaging our efforts. He never harmed a soul, even though we gave him plenty of reason to want to. I mean, you guys were fucking nuts." She stood, her temper getting the better of her. "Even when you monsters strung me up, all he did was rescue me and take care of me, not wanting to return me to the people who'd done that in the first place."

Emma took a deep breath, trying to get herself under control. "Not that I entirely blame you." She sat back down again. "None of us knew what we were getting into."

The scientist woman leaned even farther forward. "What do you mean?"

"We landed in a field of psychotropic plants. Our landing, and everything we did after that, caused the chemicals to be released, and I'm sure you all remember what happened next.

"As a measure to ensure the safety of everyone onboard, I worked with their leadership to coordinate an effort to get us off the planet. I agreed to pilot the ship off-world, and they agreed to see us off without seriously harming anyone. The worst treatment anyone received was a knock on the head to get them on the ship. They could have slaughtered us all. All we had was a small security force. They had an army.

"They agreed to allow us to leave safely and with one of their own to serve as an ambassador between their people and ours."

"You fucking cunt!" the angry man yelled, charging at her.

West reacted, grabbing him and tackling him to the ground in a maneuver that impressed Emma yet again. He'd been invaluable, changing his tune and treating her like a person. She'd been skeptical, but he really had turned over a new leaf.

"Are you all right?" he said once he had the guy under control.

"Yes, thank you."

West nodded and leaned down to the other man's ear, the one that wasn't pressed into the flooring. The other man nodded, and he let him up, poised to strike.

A loud thunk echoed off the walls, and the lights cut off. Someone shrieked, and the red emergency lights came on.

Emma jerked to a stand. "Meet me in the corridor." She looked up at the security camera, knowing Beeyun would get it. She took off at a run.

Something slammed hard behind her and she turned, laughing as Beeyun recovered from sliding into a wall at an intersection. He ran up beside her. "The ground is too slick."

"It has its advantages."

He frowned at her, and they ran side by side to the maintenance areas.

She skidded to a halt and typed in a code that unlocked the maintenance corridor. The door slid open, and she slammed into the maintenance display. "Come on, come on, come on." Her fingers danced over the screen, not touching it as she looked for the damage indicators. *Please do not let it be system-wide.*

Shouts and screamed echoed off the walls as the already stressed passengers gave in to panic, but she ignored it as a mantra echoed in her head. *Please just be lights. Please just be lights.*

"Everyone remain calm and return to your quarters," West's steady voice called down the corridor. "We are investigating the interruption in lighting and there is no reason to panic."

The noise faded to a dull roar, and Emma sighed in relief when only a single light flared red on the board. She tapped the light, bringing up the electric controls for non-essential systems. "Run pulse ping. Go."

A friendly message displayed, "Pulsing… Please wait," while she drummed her fingers against the wall. Beeyun hovered over her like an ominous shadow, cranking up the tension like mad. She wanted to tell him to calm down, but like that ever worked for anybody.

"Pulse Complete," the display read, then the window shifted to the top of the screen and a map of the non-essential electrical systems came up, highlighting in blinking red the point where the ping stopped.

"Alright. 15-Z-R. Let's go, Beeyun." She grabbed a maintenance belt from the wall next to the display and raced off to section 15, which was two intersections down from her current location.

Wires and tubing lined the walls. Big numbers the size of her hand labeled the corridor number, 13 at present, while smaller letters labeled the stack, Z being near the floor. The R stood for right, meaning the right side.

They dashed down the corridor, Beeyun having to keep his head ducked. Ordinarily, there would be no need to rush for a simple lighting issue, but she feared how the lack of light would affect everyone. Nerves already shot, she could imagine them completely losing it as the lights stayed off, preying on their minds. The dull roar of their panic teased the back of her mind, keeping her focused on the stakes.

The number changed to 14 at an intersection. After a minute or two more, it changed to 15, and they skidded to a halt. Emma dropped to her knees and ran her fingers over the clean, white tags. "Lighting, lighting, lighting." She discarded one line after the next in the Z stack until the letter L stood out to her from a line near the back. She grabbed the tag and yanked on it, pulling it away from the others. It slipped out of the stack, and she traced it with her fingers, sliding along, looking for the break.

Quarter way.

Half way.

The line pulled free, a frayed end falling to the floor in front of her. "Well, that'll do it. Where's the other end?" She dropped the line and dug her hands carefully into the bundle of wires, looking for the characteristic red and silver of high speed, copper composite.

"Can I help?" Beeyun kneeled down beside her, looking over her shoulder.

"I've got this. As long as I don't electrocute myself," she mumbled absently.

"What?" he growled.

Emma startled, banging into his chin. "Beeyun, knock it off."

"What do you mean, electrocute yourself?"

She stuck her hand back in. "Shite." An electric shock ran up her arm, leaving a tingling sensation in her fingers. She looked down but didn't see any burn marks.

"Are you all right?" Beeyun stepped forward, grabbing her hand and checking for injury.

"I'm fine, Beeyun." She shook out her hand, waving him off.

Beeyun hesitated, and she smiled at his concern, even if it wasn't warranted. He turned to stack Z, running his hands over the lines. Emma continued to shake out her hand. After a few moments, he turned around again. "Is this what you wanted?"

She nodded. "Yes. Don't touch the end."

He gave her a "Do you think I'm stupid?" look.

Emma reached in her bag and pulled out an electronic disruptor. Shaped a little like a soldering iron, she touched it to the exposed wires and waited until the in-handle display read an output of zero. She put it back and pulled out her repair tools.

"The generator's shut off power to the line. It's safe to repair now."

With a set of deft moves, she peeled the covering back, fused the wires together, and molded a new covering over it using a specialized tool with a name so long she never bothered remembering it. Something about polymer cast. She handed the line back to Beeyun. It looked like it was never damaged in the first place.

"Amazing."

Emma smirked. "It is pretty brilliant, isn't it?" She put the tools away and picked up the scraps of damaged covering, throwing the bag over her shoulder. They dashed back to the maintenance display, and she selected "Re-energize All Systems" in the upper right corner.

The lights sprang to life, and Emma smiled, but it quickly turned to a frown when she glanced down at the bits of red and silver material in her hand.

"What's wrong?"

"This doesn't make sense."

"What?"

"These look like teeth marks."

CHAPTER TWENTY-ONE

*E*mma returned to the control room, dropping into the pilot's chair with a sigh.

"Let me see your hand," Beeyun said, his voice softened with concern.

"It's fine," she said, but offered her hand to him, anyway. "More startling than anything."

He rubbed her hand and the tips of her fingers, the sensation so soothing her eyelids drifted down, her body going limp in the chair.

"Okay, that's enough." Emma pulled her hand back and started retrieving logs on the console, checking every alert since they launched. She started looking for patterns, anything that might indicate a larger issue. If there were animals on board chewing through wires, especially animals that could chew through spray-cast carbide, they needed to fix it fast. There was no telling what other damage the ship might already have.

After a few moments, she started noting repetitive shorts she wanted to investigate.

"Knock, knock," West said from the doorway.

"West," Beeyun said.

"Beeyun. Emma, what's our status?"

"Obviously, lights are back on. I'm running through sensor logs right now looking for any other potential areas for concern." Emma turned around, facing the captain with a scowl on her face. "I think we have a problem." She reached back and snatched the red and silver coverings from the console where she'd dropped them and lifted them up in her palm for West to see. "These were chewed through. I didn't think anything could chew through spray-cast carbide."

"What?" West said, looking confused.

"Not familiar with your own ships?"

"Not that familiar, I'm afraid."

Emma nodded. "Well, this stuff is fuck all expensive, pretty much only used in high end projects like space ships, and a lot of people think it's nearly indestructible. I have to use diamond-bladed cutters for repairs. But some creature on this ship chewed straight through it." She shook her head in disbelief.

West turned to Beeyun. "Any ideas? Any creatures on your planet that could do this?"

"I don't know. Your technology is different than ours. I know of some creatures with powerful jaws, some with sharp teeth. I know many of those are too big to have boarded your…" Beeyun frowned. "Ship. Ship? Yes?"

"Yes, Beeyun, ship." Emma marveled at the string of sentences that just came from her alien's mouth. Each word had been in English. When had he learned *that* much of her language?

West nodded. "What do we do?"

"We have two tasks. We need to find these creatures, and we need to fix any damage they're causing. As I said, I'm putting together a list of areas to check." Emma started waving her finger in the air as an idea came to her. She reached over to the next panel and started a heat map program. "Okay, this won't be perfect. There are too many heat sources on the ship, but it might give us an idea where best to look, and how best to hunt these bastards down."

She turned back around. "Beeyun, I want you to create a list of creatures that could be the culprits. Criteria are sharp teeth, strong jaws, and small enough to travel those maintenance corridors. We'll figure out the rest as we go."

Emma lay on her back, staring at the ceiling. Beeyun curled around her, an arm draped over her middle. She felt comfortable and safe, and part of her just wanted to roll over and bury her face in his neck before falling asleep, but she couldn't do it.

Sleep, that is.

Instead, she lay awake, staring at the boring plate metal ceiling, her mind racing over what could be wrong and what *could* go wrong. She ran her fingers absently over Beeyun's purple forearm, getting an almost hypnotic calm out of the act, like meditating or something.

Why did I tell him to come with me today?

She frowned. It had felt right in the moment, but in retrospect, her decision didn't make sense. She didn't need him to help with the repairs. In fact, he was almost a hindrance. And she hadn't been teaching him anything. So why did she want him with her? He was safer in the control room.

Emma smiled, remembering him slamming into the wall in his rush to get to her, misjudging the slick floors. She had a feeling she would be retelling that story for years to come.

The smile slowly faded as she realized she'd been relying on him more and more after returning to the ship. He was her anchor right now, keeping her grounded, connected. Which was ironic seeing as he didn't belong here. Still, Emma liked how he looked at her. She was a different person in his eyes, a better person. She didn't feel like the person he saw, but it was still flattering.

It'll never last.

Maybe if they could have stayed. Maybe on his home world, they could have made something of this, but how could they make it work now? She'd always felt like an outsider here, but Beeyun really *was* one. His skin tone was like a blazing beacon screaming, "I am other."

Emma curled up tighter, hugging herself, feeling all her fantasies crumble around her.

If only she could sleep.

If only she could just forget for a while.

Emma sat at the console the next "morning," keeping them on course as Beeyun played with the portions of the console she'd taught him how to use. They'd settled into companionable silence. Emma kept wanting to crawl into his lap and let his arms wrap around her, but the stupid designers hadn't planned for that, so they were stuck in their respective seats.

Then the constant hum that served as backdrop to their very existence cut out, leaving every surface still as a corpse.

"What was that?"

Her heart pounded in her chest. "We just lost the engines," Emma whispered, too afraid to say it with any volume. Her mind raced in panic even as her body automatically did what she could to keep them all from dying. Sub-space required constant course corrections to counter the push-pull of nearby gravity wells. Without the engines, they couldn't steer. Without the engines, they would crash into the nearest planet or star.

It was only a matter of time.

"Shite, shite, shite." She plowed some calculations into the computer, pulling data on all the nearby forces.

A timer popped up on the screen. "15:00."

14:59

14:58

"Shite!" She jumped out of her seat and ran to the door, slamming the control panel with her entire body weight. The door opened at a snail's pace, and she slipped through, scraping her back and boobs in the process, but who the fuck cared?

They were all about to die in less than fifteen minutes.

"What do I do?" Beeyun said behind her, but she ignored him. There was no time to answer.

Her soles cracked against the metal with each step, as if counting off the seconds until their doom. Emma skidded to the nearest maintenance access point. She opened the door, grabbed the tool bag, and her hands flew at speeds she didn't know they could reach as she searched for the fault on the diagnostics screen.

When the location popped up, she barely glanced at it as she raced off, clipping her shoulder on a corner. The pain screamed at her, but she ignored it. She could feel the pull of gravity, a slight shift in the way her body wanted to orient itself, telling her she wouldn't have much longer. How long had it been?

Didn't matter. All that mattered was fixing the engines and correcting their course. After reaching the engine room's antechamber, she scrambled to put on the protective gear, her hands fumbling with the closures. Once done, she fell into the engine room, barely missing a sparking, swinging line as it sailed past. Emma pressed harder into the flooring, then jumped to her feet and stared up at the room in horror. How the fuck was she going to fix this in time?

Sparks came from all directions, lines hanging haphazardly. Claw and teeth marks etched into the sides of the engines themselves, though it looked like no serious damage had been done, thank God. A few places would need patches, and a lot of lines needed fixing, but if she was fast as lightning, and God was on her side, she just might save everyone.

"What can I do to help?" Beeyun said behind her, his voice distorted.

"Gah!" She jumped, spinning around, surprised to see Beeyun in matching protective equipment. "You scared the crap out of me." Emma shook her head and pulled out a tool from her bag. "Sorry, tense. I'll fuse the lines closed. You cover them with this." It should take half the time that way. "You remember how to do this, right?" God, she hoped she wouldn't have to explain anything. They didn't have the time.

He nodded, dwarfing the tool in his big hand

Within moments, they fell into a rhythm, with the constant tone of *don't be too late, don't be too late* echoing in her mind over and over again. She couldn't think for fear of panicking, and if her mind drifted to that timer in the control room, she would just shut down entirely.

Just do your job.

Seconds clicked by, causing her heart to race, her hands to sweat and shake. Every few moments, she would have to shake out her hand as it started to hurt from holding her tools too hard. Everything felt too tense, too claustrophobic, too much. But she kept working. She couldn't stop, or they would all die.

She'd never worked like this before, and it was frying her nerves. Moments continued to pass entirely too quickly, but eventually the ever present flashes in her periphery ceased, and she moved on to sealing the breaches in the engine itself.

Another down. Another down. Another down. She kept telling herself that, not letting herself see any more than the job in front of her. If she saw how much remained, she might just break down and cry. She couldn't afford to.

Emma sat back with a flourish. "Done!" *I think.*

"What about that?"

Emma looked up, and a broken sob escaped her. A long gash ran along the ceiling on the coolant cylinder. She couldn't possibly reach it without a ladder. They didn't have time to get one. The engine would overheat and explode if the coolant cylinder wasn't fixed. "We're fucked."

CHAPTER TWENTY-TWO

*B*eeyun looked up at the damage, then down at Emma. "Not yet." He grabbed her by the thighs and hoisted her up.

Emma squealed, scrambling against the engine for balance, but calmed after a moment. Looking up, she still couldn't reach the gash. "Higher, Beeyun."

He carefully lifted her closer to the ceiling, and she rested first one foot and then the other on his shoulders. Now, the gash ran at just above chest height. Still a little high, but any higher and she would have to crane her neck against the ceiling. With the tools she still had gripped in her hands, she got to work. *Come on, come on, come on.* Why did it have to take so long?

Moments ticked by, her hands shaking and leaving the single sloppiest patch job she'd ever done in her life, but then it was done. "Down, Beeyun."

He let her down like a professional cheerleader, catching her in his arms before her feet touched the ground.

"Let's move." She needed to restart the engines and get back in the pilot's seat. The gravitational pull had grown worse, and she had to rest one hand on the wall to keep her balance. She nearly had to jump to make the turn when they reached the intersection where the diagnostics display was.

Her arm reached out for the restart button before her body was anywhere close. A nearly explosive growl echoed through the sounding chamber of the maintenance corridors as the engine started up, then it quieted down to the gentle hum they all knew so well.

"Thank Christ."

Taking off again, their feet pounded through the halls, but all Emma could think was *please don't be too late.* She had to lean harder and harder on the wall as she ran. Whatever celestial body they were nearing had almost completely countered the force of their artificial gravity systems.

Emma sailed into the control room and barked, "Move," barely registering the large body occupying the space.

A star loomed alarmingly close in the SmartScreen as she laid her hands on the controls. She banked hard. Two thumps sounded behind her, but she paid it no mind. The *Endeavour* fought her, as if begging to go visit that star, a certain siren's song. Her hands and arms strained, hurting, and she tried to force more from the ship than it had ever been designed to accomplish.

Gradually, the nose of the ship started to pull away from the sun calling it to its final resting place. Small bits of debris flew in front of them, aiming at the star as she got more and more distance between them and Death herself.

But as the ship recovered, the struggle wasn't over. Sweat slicked her palms in her protective suit as she pulled away from the star, but she had to make sure she wouldn't overcompensate, which was just as deadly. She twitched her hands and fingers in practiced movements, guiding the ship in ways she'd never had to before.

After a few more moments, the ship evened out, the forces around them let go. She let out a breath of relief. For the first time since this started, she realized she was covered in sweat. Her clothes were drenched under the protective suit. She reached up and removed the helmet, taking a much needed gasp of air. Air from the vent overhead cooled the sweat on her face. It was still hot, though. She opened up the atmospherics window. The internal temperature read 90°F.

"I tried, but we were too close to that sun." West rested a hand on the back of her chair, rubbing a spot on his hip.

She dropped the helmet to her lap, running a hand over the neckline, trying to get some airflow. "You boys okay? Sorry about the aggressive driving."

"It's not your fault. You did well, like always."

She turned around, looking at the captain. "You should check on everyone else. If you guys got banged up, I'm sure there're others in even worse shape."

West nodded and walked out the door.

"Are you okay?" she asked.

Beeyun fell into the seat next to her and smiled. "Never better."

As West made his way through the ship, his surroundings were in chaos. For the third time so far, he came upon someone cradling an injury, their head this time. "Do you need help to medical?"

The man shook his head, but groaned at the movement and didn't get up.

"Here, allow me." West reached down and lifted the injured man to his feet. He swayed for a moment before regaining his balance. "Are you sure you don't need help to medical?"

The guy almost nodded, but then said, "Yeah," instead. "That was a rough ride. Go make sure nobody else is worse."

West nodded back, waiting a moment to make sure the other man started in the right direction without falling, then continued onward. He had to walk around bits and bobs on the floor. Some were recognizable, like a fork from the mess hall, while others were little more than mangled plastic.

Time passed in weird ways, seeming to go too fast and too slow at the same time. It didn't help that he felt as unsteady on his feet as that man had looked. Between the shifts in gravity from coming dangerously close to burning up in a star and being tossed around the control room by Emma's most aggressive driving yet, he felt like someone who hadn't quite gotten his sea legs yet.

He rested a hand against the smooth wall, using it for support. People cried or moaned in the background, setting the mood as he continued through the ship. When had things gone so wrong? He'd thought they'd hit rock bottom when he and everyone around him lost all sense and control. Or maybe when Emma was forced to fly them off-world.

But things weren't improving. If anything, they seemed to be escalating. What next?

He wasn't sure he wanted to know.

Emma scratched her head, exhaustion crowding in on her as the adrenaline wore off. She stared at the blinking alerts on her display, her brain slow to process what they meant. She just wanted to curl up in her uncomfortable bed and sleep. A yawn stretched her mouth until she heard a pop in her ear.

"You're tired," Beeyun said, resting a palm on her shoulder.

She twitched her shoulder, trying to shrug him off. "Just a little more. I need to make sure we're okay."

This is ridiculous.

It was morning, for crying out loud. She shouldn't be this tired. She shook her head, trying to keep focused, awake.

Beeyun stepped in front of her and knelt down. With a single hand, he cradled her face, engulfing it. "You can't do everything, my Emma. You'll be far more effective once you've slept."

She sighed. "I wish I had your stamina." She smirked, but couldn't put the proper energy into the expression. She never realized adrenaline could affect a person so much.

"How can I help?"

She yawned again, her eyes watering. Her fingers went automatically to wipe them, then rubbed them absently. *So tired.*

"That's it." He lifted her into his arms. She didn't even have the energy to protest as he took the few steps to their bed and laid her down, wrapping her in the blankets and kissing her forehead. "Sleep sweet."

Emma woke to Beeyun hugging her side. She stretched, feeling better after getting some sleep. Beeyun mumbled, but just curled up with his eyes closed, hugging the blankets, as she slipped from bed. She smiled down at him, cherishing the rare moment of watching him sleep. Their schedules were so weird by comparison. His body was designed around a circadian rhythm equivalent to three of her days, and she suspected he got to watch her sleep far more often than she did him. Most times, he was out of bed by the time she woke.

She cracked her back, stretching her arms again as she walked toward her console. The clock showed she'd only been asleep for a few hours. It was early afternoon, but she felt fine. The short nap had done her a world of good.

She moved to the console where the heat map program had been running. "Oh, this is not good," she said as she pulled up the program. It was now running in real time, and she could see little moving heat signatures all over the ship. Most were in the maintenance corridors that housed every system keeping them alive and moving.

"Good morning, my Emma," Beeyun said, kissing her on the temple.

She jumped, surprised he could sneak up on her like that. Then again, he was Beeyun. Nothing should surprise her by now. "Good *afternoon*," she stressed. "Did you sleep well?"

"Not really. It was barely a nap."

Emma turned to him. "How long would you normally sleep?" She hadn't really thought about it, though it should have been obvious. His days *were* longer, after all. It would only make sense that he would need to sleep longer.

"Over twice as long as you usually do."

Emma frowned, concerned. How could this possibly work when his entire life was on a different schedule than hers? She didn't know, and it hurt her heart a little thinking of it. Maybe they couldn't make it work. Maybe they were doomed.

And here he'd left his planet behind. Was it because he was ordered to, or was it for her? Fear tightened her chest. She felt responsible, like she'd taken something from him and now was solely responsible for keeping him happy.

She didn't know if she could.

CHAPTER TWENTY-THREE

*S*parks flew, startling the creatures as they moved around the hostile territory. Predators tricked and deceived here, scentless but equally deadly. The scent of dead and burnt flesh drifted on the air. They moved onward.

The little creature jumped to the side, avoiding a white leaf with black markings. Sparks flew beside it, the result of one of it's compatriots looking for food and finding only death once again.

A spark arced across the room, startling it into yet another direction, away from a chewed and frayed line. It was hungry, starving, but while it sensed heat, potential food sources all around, all they found were cold not-food and hot death.

It was getting weak. It had to find something to eat... fast.

They walked to get some food after waking from their nap. The aftermath of the recent events still littered the halls, and Emma carefully maneuvered around debris. People didn't talk to them, didn't look at them funny, didn't glare either. No one tried to pick a fight or tell them they didn't belong. As they entered the mess hall, it was quiet. Too quiet.

The room was the most populated place she'd been since returning. It should be loud. There should be people talking, and yet as they stood in the doorway, the only noises were utensils scraping on plates and food crunching in mouths. Emma was tense as she and Beeyun collected trays and sat to eat, expecting to be bothered, but they weren't. It didn't feel like acceptance, but maybe tolerance at least. Tolerance was a good first step.

They ate in companionable silence and walked back to the control room holding hands, his warm palm relaxing her, making the problems they faced seem a little more manageable. She unlocked the door and stalled, eyes going wide at the chaotic sea of flashing lights on the console.

She dashed forward, daunted and unsure where to start. The world paused, holding its breath in the moment before everything fell apart.

An alarm went off over her head, and she cringed. She leaned over the console, silencing alarms so she could think. "We just lost life support."

"What's that?" Beeyun asked behind her back, for once not crowding her.

"What it sounds like. Space is harsh. Those systems keep us comfortable, keep us breathing. The systems have certain fail safes, but it won't help for long."

Emma hovered over the console, trying to pinpoint the problem. "Come on," she said to herself, her finger hovering in the air as she searched. "There!" Spotting the issue, she jammed her finger at the indicator in triumph before turning and running for the door.

She didn't look back to see if he followed.

Captain West stopped on the other side, and she almost barreled into him. "What the hell just happened?"

"We lost life support."

"I can see *that*," he said, sarcasm dripping from his voice as he crossed his arms over his chest.

She didn't have time for his attitude, could barely even process it. "Good, then you can help me fix it."

Assuming it *was* fixable. Her mind sniped at her, throwing out worst-case scenarios that seemed to just keep happening in real life.

Please let it be fixable.

Emma collapsed into the pilot's chair, her heart still racing from fear and lack of oxygen. Her hands shook as they hovered over the life support system. She wasn't built for this. It was too much. Too much responsibility, too much stress.

Beeyun stood behind her, his constant touch sinking in, soothing her. She closed her eyes, letting the butterfly touches take away the stress and tension. Her mind started to clear from the crazy fog that had built with each moment they'd inched closer to destruction. She wanted to go home, curl up in bed, and never come out. If Beeyun was beside her, all the better.

As her mind continued to clear, a half-stupid thought bubbled up. She laughed.

"What's so funny?" the captain growled.

She'd forgotten he was there. "I just thought of this line from this movie I like, Tremors II."

"I've never heard of it." And from the way the captain's shoulders tensed, he had no interested in hearing about it.

"They had just learned something about the monster creatures in the story. They were attracted to heat, killing vehicles, communications equipment, and whatnot. Someone, I can't remember his name, commented about the creatures being so smart because they were so dumb." She laughed, barely putting any effort into it. She was emotionally drained.

"Maybe they are," Beeyun said, his hands stilling.

"Explain," the captain snapped at Beeyun, glaring for good measure.

Beeyun feared his language skills would not be up to this task. He could speak in fairly good sentences, but some of the words he only knew in his tongue, others he suspected had no correlation. "I will try." He looked to Emma, worried for her. If the creature on this ship was what he suspected, they would be hard-pressed to survive this.

"I need to see them to know for certain, but I have suspicions. There is a creature on my planet, highly destructive, attracted to heat. They are small, so they could slip onto the ship undetected, but I would need to see one to know for sure."

Emma stood up. "Then we find one, catch one. We need to know what we're up against. I can use the heat map to find them."

The captain nodded. "Excellent. Let's get hunting."

"One sec," Emma said, pulling a tablet out of a charging dock. She moved her fingers over it, then hovered over the console. "I've just got to sync the heat map program to my device."

"Good," the captain said. "Emma, you direct us with the tablet. Beeyun, follow and keep your head on a pivot. You're the only one who knows what we're looking for."

"Of course," Beeyun said, settling in behind his Emma as they returned to the maintenance level once more. After three previous trips down there, he almost felt familiar with the alien landscape. He'd never imagined anything like it in his life, let alone expected to one day see it. It seemed ludicrous to be comfortable with it, but he was starting to become numb to it all, at least.

Always living as one with nature, he couldn't imagine anyone building such a monstrosity, something so hakkan. It defied logic, his every belief and virtue. But he kept quiet, knowing it wasn't his place to judge this culture, this people, on their own turf.

He wanted to ask Emma what her home world was like. Was it like this spaceship? Devoid of all things natural, a sea of mechanical menaces that left him cold inside? He hoped not.

Emma walked in front of him, but he could see over her bent head as she walked with the device in her hands. It reminded him of the tablet in his own home, except it looked like every other machine in this society.

Not being able to help himself, he hovered over her, feeling protective, wanting to be between her and any threat. He couldn't do that from behind her, which gnawed at him. He wanted to hide her away, protect her, but there was nowhere to go. The danger was everywhere. Nowhere on the ship was safe until they fixed this.

They walked deeper into the ship at her guidance. He could see her tablet, but couldn't figure out where she was leading. Heat signatures overwhelmed the screen, so what was she looking for? He didn't understand any of it. Everything around him was alien, strange. He couldn't even imagine the world that awaited him. In his gut, he knew it would be nothing like his own. He drew a blank when he tried to picture it.

But more than that, he was afraid for the future, afraid Emma would turn from him, that she would eventually see all their differences and decide it was too much. He saw all of them. How could he not? Their skin color and disparate heights were the least of their differences, but it didn't matter to him. He needed to be with her.

Around them, the white noise he'd dismissed as one of the many things he didn't understand, and didn't want to ponder, grew. After a while, he realized it wasn't white noise but skittering. The rapid steps of the creatures surrounded them, and his stomach sank, knowing they were close to their goal.

Please don't let it be them.

He couldn't think of a single way to get rid of those little vermin if they'd infiltrated the ship. On his home world, it had taken entire armies of hunters to wipe the things out. They had developed techniques of guarding heat sources, but the little beasts had brought entire cities nearly to starvation and destruction repeatedly through their history.

He couldn't imagine they had the resources on this ship necessary to exterminate the little monsters. He didn't know much about this place, but he knew they were in over their heads.

Emma lifted her hand to stop them, and Beeyun settled in behind her without a word. She paused for a moment, then pointed near the wall before her. Darkness surrounded them in this part of the corridor. He couldn't see anything except her tablet and the area it illuminated.

But he could hear, and there was a creature close by. Beeyun nudged Emma to the side, walking in front of her. He didn't make a sound, taking each step with care as his claws descended slowly and smoothly. He felt the captain's alarm at his back. A couple more steps and he could hear the little menace's rapid heartbeat. He crouched, waiting, ready.

The thing skittered, stopped, skittered some more. It seemed fearless, but Beeyun couldn't see the walls, didn't know if he could reach the creature yet. It started to move toward him, the tiny nails tapping at the metal surfaces. He flexed his hand, ready.

Snap.

He dug deep, tightening his claws around the little furry body. Wetness coated his fingers, and it squealed, squirming and thrashing before going still. He lifted it up in his hand, but he couldn't see it in the near perfect darkness. "I need some light to get a look at it."

"Sure, follow me," Emma said. She stepped around the captain and led them back to the control room, her tablet lighting the way.

Blood plopped down to the floor below their feet as he walked, the coppery smell filling his nostrils. He didn't look down even when he could. He hoped he was wrong and didn't really want confirmation.

One step after the next, he focused on the back of Emma's head as they passed into a section that was better lit. Beeyun found comfort in seeing her in front of him, safe for the moment. He could sense the panic of the people around him, but ignored it. He didn't care.

They arrived at the control room, and the captain closed the door behind them.

"So, what is it?" the man said, crossing his arms over his chest, as if the puny appendages could intimidate him. Or was that a defense mechanism?

Beeyun brought the little beast up, still impaled on his claws. He wasn't able to bring himself to do so before, some part of him knowing what he would see. "Ayat," he said, confirming his worst fears.

"Wait," Emma said, surprised. "Doesn't that mean to eat?"

"The base of the word does, yes. These creatures are known for eating everything in sight. They are attracted to heat first, but they're scavengers, and will eat almost anything."

"Including metal?" the captain said, incredulous, his arms dropping to his sides.

"Our building materials aren't like yours, but they have been known to eat anything stationary that generates heat, even non-animate objects."

They all fell quiet, uneasiness filling the room.

"With this on the ship, I'm not sure we can get rid of them. As long as they have something to eat, they will replicate."

"But how are they finding nutrients? They're eating metal, for crying out loud!" Emma threw up her hands, frustrated.

"They aren't actually *eating* it. The damage is likely a side effect, like with that movie you mentioned. They are indiscriminate, biting into anything they come across. Sometimes, they bite down to test if it is food, to eat, or even get at a suspected food source. They are perfectly capable of chewing through a wall to reach their target."

Emma paled, and he wanted to reach out to her, comfort her. "We can't let them get to Earth," she said, standing frozen.

"No, we can't," the captain agreed. "I'll organize a hunt to get rid of these creatures."

"Can we seal off the maintenance layers and vent it?" Emma said.

"Maybe, but that's dangerous as well. Look, it's my responsibility to formulate a plan. Leave it to me, okay? You just focus on piloting the ship." His voice was almost pleading.

Emma tensed, a variety of emotions crossing her face as she stood there. Then she nodded and turned toward the console at her back. Beeyun leaned forward, wanting to learn, to know what she was going to do. It was on the tip of his tongue to ask. She leaned over the console, touching it, and a red haze tinted the window.

"What have you done?" the captain yelled, dashing toward the console, anger and shock in his form.

Beeyun jumped, and Emma turned around, arms crossed over her chest, lifting her chin defiantly. "What I had to do."

CHAPTER TWENTY-FOUR

*E*mma stood her ground as the captain gave her a death glare. "I activated the Ecological Quarantine protocol."

Behind her, red letters flashed on the screen. Beeyun couldn't read them, but he assumed they echoed her foreign words.

"Fuck. You're not authorized to do that. *I'm* the captain!"

The captain pointed his finger in Emma's face, and Beeyun bristled, but held still, not wanting to create an incident. The captain wasn't trying to harm Emma. She was in no danger from him.

"What does that mean?" Beeyun asked.

Emma turned to him. "Sorry, Beeyun. New words. Quarantine means that no one and nothing can leave the ship. Ecological Quarantine is used when there is an organism on board that would be a threat if released on Earth."

Beeyun nodded, feeling better about this trip. That they had such a protocol meant he may have misjudged them when calling them hakkan. They weren't the same as his people, didn't respect nature equally, but they must respect it somewhat or they wouldn't have such a protocol.

"I'll have your wings when this is over, pilot," the captain snarled.

Emma leaned toward him, her own finger now in his face as well. "Try it. I dare you. I followed the rules. This thing is a threat to Earth. You try telling them we shouldn't have activated the quarantine, and *you'll* be the one up on charges."

The captain paused, his face tight with anger, turning an alarming shade of red. With a sharp movement, he turned away from Emma and toward Beeyun. "Tell me everything you know about these creatures."

"Ordinarily, they aren't a sufficient threat. They live in areas where resources are either scarce or seasonal, which controls their population size. There are also often sufficient predators to keep them in line. The problems lie when they get too close to civilization. Predators become rarer, resources more plentiful, and their population soars.

"We've engineered methods of keeping them away."

"How?" the captain barked.

"Natural barriers, mostly."

The captain frowned.

"In the past, when they got too close, we had to organize hunts. It was not easy since there are more resources around habitations, so they reproduce as fast as we kill them."

"Well, there's limited resources on this ship," Emma said thoughtfully, rubbing her chin.

"Can we trap them somehow? Draw them to a kill zone?" the captain said, his anger having faded.

"It's not easy. They need to have no access to other food sources. That includes food we would consume, people, animals, or most anything organic. Even then, it will be hard to draw them exactly where we want."

"So we need a large source of heat with no distractions," Emma chimed in.

"Shit," the captain said, shaking his head. "I've never thought about how many sources of heat exist in this ship. How are we going to isolate them to one place?"

"Well, we can shut down almost every system. Problem is, life support requires circulating air, which would circulate heat around the ship." Emma touched her lips, thinking.

"Let's regroup in the morning. Emma, do an inventory of all the emergency breathers on the ship. Also, analyze the ship for insulated rooms."

"The only one I can think of at the moment is the ice box."

He narrowed his eyes at her.

"Fine," she said, raising her hands up in surrender. "I'll do it. Hopefully, we can find something better."

Emma had downloaded a record of all the emergency breathers, along with their locations. She walked through the ship, documenting each one, checking them off as she went. She'd also downloaded the specs on every room on the ship, looking at wall densities, insulating materials, and such. So far, the only other room she'd found with insulating capacities was the engine room.

But that room was insulated for a reason. The engines, when running at full capacity, could output enough heat to turn the interior of the room into an oven. In fact, they used the heat output from that room to power the oven and heat the rest of the ship by controlling airflow.

She frowned.

"Is everything well?" Beeyun asked behind her.

"I think I found a room for our needs, but I have no idea how long it will take to drop the temperature to acceptable conditions for humans, well, us." She switched to a spreadsheet program. Using the room size, insulation, and capacity for temperature dispersion, she estimated the time it would take to cool the room to about one hundred degrees Fahrenheit. Her college courses were suddenly really coming in handy.

"Bloody hell." Three days.

She drummed her fingers on the back of the tablet. They needed to vent the heat from the room faster. Ordinarily, they never did that. When maintenance was required, the techs wore special suits designed to protect them from the extreme temperatures, suits they'd used earlier that day, in fact.

Could she vent it into space? But that would sacrifice oxygen, resources she would rather not lose if she could help it.

She pulled up some more quick calculations, this time calculating a dispersion the size of the ship, not just that small room. It would temporarily increase the temperature in the ship to a hundred and five, but the room would drop to habitable levels within two hours. She smiled. It would also mask the residents from the rodents' senses. Human body temperature was lower and would just blend in, allowing them to mobilize, put a plan in action.

"Got it. It'll take a couple of hours, but it should work."

She switched back to the list of breathers and continued checking each one off.

Emma paced the small control room, lightly touching the cold metal wall each time she turned. She had to walk around their bed on the floor, around the chairs, even around Beeyun, but she just couldn't sit still. There was too much going on, too much at stake. In her mind, all those bright red dots from the heat map program kept taunting her, haunting her.

We might not make it.

I *might not make it.*

She looked over at Beeyun sitting in one of the chairs. He'd been watching her, but hadn't said a word, giving her the space she needed. What would she do without him? Whether he realized it or not, he was her rock, giving her the strength she needed right now.

She didn't want to be strong, though. If anything, she wanted to curl up in a ball and never leave. She was a pilot, an engineer. She'd never imagined being in this situation before. Hell, she couldn't remember even an Emergency Training drill that covered this specific scenario.

I shouldn't have come.

Emma had a family back home, parents. It wasn't much, maybe less than most, but it was certainly more than some. Sure, she'd always felt like an outcast, an outsider, like she never belonged, but whose fault was that? Everyone had the opportunity to fit in somewhere. Everyone had a value somewhere. Hell, she was a world-class pilot, for crying out loud! She was an engineer. She had skills. She had merit.

"I have value," she mouthed, stopping her pacing.

And I really *need to stop looking for others for validation.*

If she was being honest with herself, she should have never taken this assignment. Emma had only recently become a pilot, had barely gotten her feet wet. She'd only done a few dozen shuttle runs to the space station or Kennedy Moon Station before being offered this assignment. She should have declined, tried to settle into her role as a pilot. But wasn't that just her way? As soon as she'd turned eighteen, she'd left home, deciding she was going to become an engineer. Then, as soon as she got her degree, did she try to find an engineering job? No, she decided she would become a pilot. And she convinced herself it was a logical progression, a logical next step.

But it wasn't. She'd graduated, but instead of feeling a sense of accomplishment, she'd felt lost, still searching for… something. She supposed that was why she leapt on this assignment, eager to start. But it was stupid, illogical, to think this would be different. Emma wouldn't find what she was looking for in a temporary assignment like this. After all, the crew were supposed to leave after the site was set up. It was a long assignment, but she'd been deluding herself if she'd ever thought she could connect with these people. She was setting herself up for failure every time she hoped for them to accept her, to like her. It would have always ended in tragedy, at least for her. Eventually, she would have flown away.

Not that she regretted coming. She looked at Beeyun again. She would have regretted not meeting him.

Emma paused, a nagging thought preying on her. She frowned, trying to suss it out.

Fly away.

She was the only one who could fly this ship home. She didn't know how serious this threat was. Obviously, if they didn't kill these creatures, they could never return to Earth, but was that it? Or did they pose a more dangerous threat? What if one of them was killed by the little bastards? What if *she* was killed?

Her hands tensed at her sides. If she died, could they ever get home? Did anyone else know how to control the ship? Maybe the captain knew a little, but he'd also literally had to ask her to send broadcasts across the ship. Would he know how to send a TAT message, send for help?

Emma crossed the room, taking her seat. "Here, Beeyun. Pay attention. I'm going to show you a few things about the ship."

Just in case.

"Well?" Captain West said first thing the next morning, arms crossed as he sat in the control room.

"I have a plan." Sort of. "There are enough breathers for everyone. And there is one other room we can use to mask our body heat. The engine room. If we shut off the engines, then vent the heat across the ship, it'll take two hours to drop the temperature low enough."

"But won't that super-heat the ship environment?" West said.

Emma shrugged. They could deal with a little heat. "It'll get hot. People will be sweating, but it'll be manageable. It will also mask our body heat and maybe even other minor sources of heat, which will limit the ayat. We'll need to shut off any device that outputs heat anywhere close to body heat or above."

He nodded. "We'll need something to draw them, then."

Or would they? She turned to Beeyun. "Would the combined body heat of the security team be enough to draw them?"

Beeyun didn't answer immediately. "How hot would the air temperature be?"

Emma frowned. "Well, at first, well above body temperature, but once the engine room is habitable, we'll stop venting it, and the air should start cooling down."

"Well, once the ayat can sense bodies, I don't see why that wouldn't work."

"And with everyone else in the engine room behind all that insulation, they should only go to one place. We just have to make sure no other heat sources can draw them."

"Do you have a list of things to shut off?"

"No," Emma said, hesitating as she realized she'd missed something. "I'll get right on that."

"Good," West said, nodding. "You collect that information, and we'll meet in the mess hall to finalize the plan."

"Yes, sir."

est stood tall at one end of the mess hall. The large room was mostly empty, only containing him, the security team, the pilot, and her alien friend. He could hear grumbling in the hall from people wanting to eat lunch. He should have thought of that before scheduling this meeting for noon.

The security team were restless and angry, still holding a grudge over him setting them in their places. Fortunately, they were being professional about it and weren't letting their emotions get the better of them anymore. They stood at the back of the room, far away from Emma and Beeyun.

"Let's get started. If you don't already know, we are currently under an ecological quarantine." He couldn't help himself, his gaze turning to glare on Emma for a moment before pulling himself back to the task at hand. "There is an alien pest species on board the ship. In order to lift the quarantine, we need to eliminate this threat."

"Shit," someone said from the back of the room, stomping his foot.

"What does this mean?" one of the others said.

"No one can leave the ship until the threat is resolved."

The security team stood taller, losing some of their tension, a sense of purpose filling them up like air in a balloon.

"Beeyun, would you care to explain the situation?"

The big purple alien bowed and stood. "The ayat are an invasive species. They are attracted to heat and are extremely destructive. They've shown themselves capable of eating through metal and your more sensitive systems. They are the reason for the problems you've had of late." He nodded and sat.

"Thank you, Beeyun. Here is the plan. We are going to shut off the engines, venting the heat across the ship. We'll then turn off any heat sources flagged by our pilot. Once the engine room temperature is habitable, all but myself and the security team will lock themselves inside. *We* will station ourselves in the cargo bay and wait for the temperature to drop enough for our body temperatures to be visible by the ayat. That should be enough to attract them and give us an adequate kill zone."

"Won't it get hot?"

Emma stood and turned to the security team. "Yeah, my calculations say it'll take two hours to get the engine room cool enough to enter without special equipment. By that time, the ship air temperature will be around 105 degrees Fahrenheit."

"Any more questions?"

Silence answered as everyone looked at each other.

"All right, let's get to work!"

Emma shut the engines down once they reached normal space, a little unnerved by the eerie quiet that followed. She didn't like it, didn't like being stationary. It felt too much like being broken down, stuck, trapped. That something was wrong only made the feeling worse.

She looked to Beeyun, calm and stoic at her side. Was he unafraid or simply didn't know enough about what was going on. "Come on." She grabbed her tablet, which she'd downloaded the life support system controls to. Now, she could monitor and control the systems remotely, which they would need. She needed to keep a close eye on room temperatures, make sure nothing got out of hand.

She felt nervous, afraid she'd made a mistake in her calculations. What if it got too hot? What if she'd miscalculated and the engine room took too long to cool off? What if it *didn't* cool off? She still could vent the room, if needed.

With a few taps on the screen, she changed the airflow patterns, running the air completely through the engine room. The ventilation hissed as it kicked on and hot air blasted her, ruffling her hair a bit. It felt good, soothing. For a moment, she didn't want to move, just wanted to soak in the heat.

But soon her brow was sweating, and she stepped out of the airflow. "We've got to go to the engine room antechamber." They'd gathered most of the breathers in the antechamber and commanded all but the security team to gather there. She figured she and Beeyun would be the last ones there. The engines couldn't be shut off anywhere but at the control room. Well, that and inside the engine room, but why send someone in there when the engines were running unless it was absolutely necessary.

Everything was quiet as she walked briskly through the halls. They felt evacuated, abandoned, which she suspected was exactly what would happen if they didn't stop these beasts. Beeyun hadn't said it, but she suspected that once they no longer had other sources of food, they would go after the crew, the passengers. If they didn't do something soon, they wouldn't survive long enough to reach Earth.

A chill ran down her spine at the thought, and her steps quickened.

What if they failed?

What if the security team couldn't get them all?

She tried to shrug those worries aside, but they persisted. They wouldn't go away, tormenting her every few moments with possibilities. There were far more ways this could go wrong than ways it could go right, and she knew it. *She'd* been the one the captain had gone to for information. She knew futility surrounded them.

Emma couldn't see past this. Perhaps that was why she was a pilot and not a captain. He constantly chastised her for over-reaching her position, but she didn't want his role, didn't want the responsibility. She wanted to know that someone else was handling it, someone else would keep them safe, alive. Did that make her a coward?

It made her something, and she wasn't sure she liked what it said about her. She stopped in front of the antechamber. A cacophony of voices came from the other side. She pushed it open and every one of the passengers and crew, other than the captain and security team, stood crowded together in a room too small for their number.

Ordinarily, the antechamber held a maximum of a half dozen people. Usually, though, there were only two. One person entered the engine room while the other stayed in the antechamber, waiting by the comm to help if needed. As one of the most dangerous places in the ship, safety was essential.

"Lacy," she said, spotting her friend.

"Emma," her friend said, rushing over. "What's happening? We were just told to come here."

Tempted, she almost said, "You don't want to know," but she held her tongue. "The security team is working on solving the problem."

"What problem? Is this related to the engines and life support going down?"

She nodded. "We have stowaways that are wrecking havoc on the systems. We need to control heat signatures so we can draw them to a single location to get rid of them. It'll take a few hours, but that should be the end of it."

As she looked around, though, she wondered if so many people crammed into such a small space would survive several hours.

———

Something was changing. The creature sensed more and more moving food sources nearby. It skittered around, joined by more of its kind. It felt the brushing of fur against fur. One of them snapped sharp teeth, and it snapped back.

They stopped when an obstacle got in their way, but hungry, they were determined to get at the food. They started scratching at the walls, their sharp claws making slow work of the material unlike any they'd ever encountered before. It didn't like this place, missed open fields and easy, if scarce, prey. This place was cold, hard, and prey was hard to reach and even scarcer.

It was so hungry.

It just wanted to eat.

———

"I've had it," a male voice yelled, stomping as he crossed the room.

The temperature in the engine room had dropped low enough to enter a half hour ago, but instead of the larger room soothing their frayed nerves, it only exacerbated them. Emma monitored Life Support systems on her tablet, but there was little she could do at the moment.

It was still hot, and everyone looked a little bedraggled. There wasn't a single dry shirt in the group, dark sweat stains covered backs, armpits, and anywhere skin came close to skin. Emma lifted her clinging shirt away from her skin, waving it to get some airflow, make herself feel a little cooler. Multiple times now, she'd had to wipe her brow before sweat dripped in her eyes. She'd never been so hot in her life.

She shook off her distraction. "You can't leave," Emma said, stepping in front of the man and holding her hand up at chest level.

"Try to stop me," he said, leaning into her personal space, face mottled red with anger and the effects of the heated space.

"We have to stay here until the captain gives the all clear."

"We've already been trapped for hours." He leaned forward, his face getting redder. Then his eyes widened, his face blanching.

Emma frowned, but then felt Beeyun pressed behind her. He wrapped his arms around her, but as she looked down, she saw that his claws were out. No wonder the other man had blanched.

"Please find a place to sit, relax. We're all stuck here. Just be patient a little while longer." Emma pleaded with the man, with all of them, really. This was a stressful situation, but they couldn't just go off the rails. They needed to see it through.

As she leaned back into Beeyun, she noticed all eyes on her. Or maybe on him. They all seemed uneasy, and Emma wondered if they'd just taken a huge step back in him being accepted by the others.

West waited with a rifle pressed to his shoulder, his men behind him. How much longer would they have to wait? Emma had said it would take two hours for the engine heat to flood the ship. But how long would it take for the ayat to sense the concentrated heat signature of him and his men?

Air seemed to circulate differently in the cargo bay of the *Endeavour*. When they were shutting off devices from the pilot's list, it had been brutal, the vents blasting them with heat every time they passed one. He couldn't tell if this was better or worse, though. There was little or no air circulation in the cargo bay. People weren't intended to be in here very often, so the systems focused on keeping other areas of the ship comfortable. The upside? They didn't have blasts of heat hitting them regularly. The downside? The air just sat around them, sweltering and intolerable.

Around him, the members of the security team paced, weapons at the ready even though they still had time before the temperature dropped low enough. It made them feel better. He knew it did for him. With a sigh, he dropped his rifle and pulled out his comm. "Emma, what's our status?"

"Hello, Captain." He frowned. There was a smile in her voice. "Temperature's about a hundred degrees."

His frown grew. They still had some time to wait, and he grew more concerned the longer they stood at attention. He was worried they would get sloppy, especially in this heat. That was why they had been taking ten minute shifts, with half his men on watch while the other half relaxed. He wouldn't risk any of them not being ready when the time came.

Unfortunately, none of them could truly relax when they were not "on shift."

How much longer could they go on like this?

CHAPTER TWENTY-SIX

The creature spun around in confusion. Heat surrounded it on all sides. It snapped at the open air, but connected with nothing. Eventually, it either adjusted to the higher temperature, which made it irritable and aggressive, or the temperature reduced. It couldn't tell which, it was so disoriented.

Everything around it was the same, with no variation. It continued on, feeling with its teeth, but nothing seemed like food. It vocalized it its stress, its fellow beings replying in kind.

It sniffed the air, listened for sounds, anything. At first, the noise of the rest of its kind drowned out anything else. Skittering feet and vocalizations much like its own filled the air. The scent of spilled blood ran thick in its nostrils, but the blood was old, and it crawled across the wet floor as something new teased its weaker senses.

There was a sound, like many prey moving at once. It was in the same direction as a teasing smell it couldn't identify. Its nose was useless to identify food, but whatever it heard, it was *moving*.

It was *food*.

<hr>

Emma sat with Beeyun at her back, nestled between his thighs as he curled his arms around her. Though it was hot in the engine room, his body heat soothed her. Glancing around, many of the other occupants could use the same comfort. People paced and grumbled, nerves frayed to their limits by the long imprisonment.

It didn't seem to matter to them that it was necessary. They didn't seem to care that if they didn't get these creatures off the ship, none of them would ever leave. She supposed that was the problem with traveling with civilians. Certainly, military personnel wouldn't act that way. Though she wouldn't change things to save her life, she suddenly wished their crew had been military, instead.

"Fuck this," a man said, rushing for the door.

"No," Emma said, jumping and stumbling as she got to her feet. But in the time it took her to stand, the door was already open.

Time stood still. She waited with bated breath, then time clicked back into motion, and she raced forward to close the door. She reached it, pressing her palm to the insulated metal door, but it jerked out of her hand as a swarm of cat-sized rodents raced through, slamming it open.

CHAPTER TWENTY-SEVEN

ehind her, someone screamed, "Close the door!"

But it was too late for that. She knew it. Beeyun reached down, slicing at the beasts as they flowed into the room, shrieks and cries serenading them. Emma put her entire bodyweight into trying to keep the door closed, shoving her shoulder against the unyielding metal. Her world narrowed to the task at hand. It took all her strength, all her focus, just to keep the door ajar, but even then, she could feel the small bodies pounding against the other side, could see the occasional one slip through.

"I can't do this." Her muscles were hurting, straining with the force needed to hold the little beasts at bay. And to think they'd called Beeyun "The Beast."

A purple hand slapped the door next to her arm. "I've got this."

She looked up at him. As she eased back, he pushed all his weight against the door, closing the gap, but not quite able to close the door so they could lock it. With a little more force, she suspected they would be safe, that they could close and lock it. Her hand went to the door, but then stopped.

Her mouth opened, but words didn't come out at first. "I think I have an idea."

"Well, do it already!" someone yelled behind her. She turned around, taking in all the scared, traumatized faces. She nodded and crossed the few feet to her tablet and picked it up. "West, you read?"

"Loud and clear, Emma. What's the situation?"

"The ayat are here."

"What?!"

She flinched at the distorted audio. "Some got in, but Beeyun killed them. I think we can keep them focused on us. How fast can your team get to the antechamber?"

"How many entrances does it have?"

"Just two. Unlike the maintenance corridors, it has solid walls just like other rooms on the ship. I think if we can keep them focused on our door, we can keep them here until you arrive."

"Good idea. We're on the way. Just hold tight."

Emma felt useless as Beeyun stood lazily against the door while little paws with terrifyingly sharp claws slipped through the crack, trying to do damage, to enter. His body bobbed back and forth as the ayat slammed against the door behind him.

I should have taught West how to control the ship.

What if she died here? What if she was incapacitated? What if one of those things got in here and got her? She'd told

Beeyun enough so he could call for emergency assistance from Earth, but he was in here too. What were the chances she would get hurt, and he wouldn't? Hell, with how protective he was of her, he would probably get hurt trying to save her.

Watching her, he lifted his hand, gesturing for her to approach. She did, and he curled an arm around her, his deadly claws coated in blood as they pressed gently against her tender flesh. "What's wrong?" he said.

"What if it all goes wrong?" She looked up at him. "We're the only ones on the ship who know how to send a message to Earth. I'm the only one who can fly this thing."

He pressed her closer to him, leaning his face against her forehead. "Nothing is going to happen to you. I won't allow it. Hell, neither will the captain. He knows what he's doing."

She looked at him, puzzled. "I didn't think you liked humans."

He shrugged. "I like a few."

She laughed. "I like a few, too."

The door to the engine room antechamber was open as West and his team approached. Light spilled out into the darker maintenance corridor. With hand signals, he coordinated his team, leaving several behind to kill any that tried escaping. With the rest, he charged forward, weapon at the ready.

They surged in as the little beasts scratched frantically at the engine room door. Deep gouges had been torn into the metal. The door bobbed as their cat-sized bodies slammed against it.

Someone's holding it closed.

He opened fire, the cracks of gunfire echoing off the walls in the small chamber. Using a gun on a ship was always a last resort, and not just because it could pierce the hull. With the rooms so small, sound carried and amplified. They didn't have earplugs, hadn't anticipated taking on their enemy in such a small space.

With the first shot, the beasts scattered, surging around the room. His men called out, trying to be heard over the weapons fire as they coordinated efforts.

Aim. Shoot. Aim. Shoot.

His gun swiveled, trying to keep up with the little bastards. His heart pounded in his chest, and he felt deaf, his ears ringing after so many gunshots. Blood splattered the walls and little bodies were piling up in the small room, making it increasingly difficult to outmaneuver them. They were fast and agile. He, on the other hand, tripped over one of their deceased, slamming into the nearest wall.

A brown body leapt at him, going for his leg. "Fuck!" he screamed, swinging his gun barrel down to try to dislodge it. Pain seared his leg where it latched on. "Get the fuck off!" He could barely hear his own words, but the ayat certainly didn't let go. He beat it with his gun, but its sharp nails dug in, slicing into him further.

"Gotcha, Captain," a muffled voice said, raising his weapon and firing.

The creature went limp, dead. He peeled it off. "Thanks." He doubted the other man could hear him.

Putting both hands on his gun again, he sighted, searching for his next target, but they were thinning. There were fewer live ayat in the room than humans. A few more moments, and the sound of gunshots ceased, making the ringing in his ears deafening.

He limped to the door, looking out at the men he'd stationed there. "Are we clear?"

"Aye, sir," they both said.

He nodded, moving back to the engine room door. He knocked two times. "It's safe."

The door peeked open, a purple face streaked with blood staring back at him. The alien's gaze dropped to the floor littered with bodies and nodded, opening the door the rest of the way. Emma hugged his side. Behind them, a collection of dead creatures littered the floor and everyone else hugged the far wall, too afraid to come closer.

West turned to Emma. "Check for heat signatures on the ship. I want to see if there's any more of these."

She nodded. "Yes, Captain." She leaned away from her alien, checking her tablet.

West leaned off his injured leg, the sharp pain distracting him as blood ran down his calf.

Her fingers continued to run over the device's surface. "There are still heat signatures around the ship, but I can't tell if they're ayat. Nothing big, though. So, I would say, if there are any left, they're probably not in groups."

West nodded. "Stay on the comm. I want you to direct us to these heat signatures so we can check them out. I want to eliminate them one by one."

"Yes, sir."

Emma sat on the floor of the engine room. The security team had swept the room, making sure none of the creatures remained before checking the rest of the ship. Once they left,

Beeyun kicked all the dead bodies into the antechamber. There was little they could do about the blood pools and smears right now.

Her ears were still ringing from the gunfire, which had echoed through the engine room during the fight. She'd wanted to cover her ears, but hadn't wanted to relinquish her hold on Beeyun either.

He touched her shoulder, and she jerked her head up to look at him. "Are you all right?" His voice was muffled, almost silent, and it took her a second to piece together what he'd said.

She nodded, and he sat down next to her, curling an arm around her shoulders. Emma sat with her tablet propped on her knees, waiting on the captain's next request. She'd directed him to the first location. Now, she ran her fingers over the smooth edge of the device, distracting herself with the sensation.

"Clear," he said over the comm. "It's a device charging in someone's room. I've disconnected it from the wall."

"Good. The next heat source is two rooms over."

She felt good about this. They'd turned off a lot of heat sources on the ship in anticipation of their first botched plan. Now, hours later, the temperature was starting to feel more bearable, though it was still pretty hot. Sweat clung to her, unable to cool her off in the stagnant air. It would take hours before the temperature came even close to normal. By then, they could check each heat source, eliminate it as a potential threat. They could do this.

I can do this.

CHAPTER TWENTY-EIGHT

---

*B*eeyun felt wrung out after the day they'd had. By the time the captain released Emma from her duty, she was dead on her feet, swaying in place after he helped her stand. It was starting to get cool on the ship, though he couldn't say if that was because he'd become used to the heat after surviving it all day.

"I'm fine," Emma said, yawning so widely it looked like half her face would break off.

"Emma, you're exhausted."

She shook her head. "Fine," she mumbled, but her feet shuffled forward. She didn't even have the energy to lift them.

He lifted her into his arms. "You're not fine. You're exhausted. I'm taking you to bed."

A silly smile crossed her face. "Promises, promises."

He paused, suspecting he was missing some sort of nuance. She'd seemed adamant that she was fine, that she didn't need assistance, that she wasn't exhausted, and yet her words made him think she looked forward to sleep?

The concern slipped from his mind as Emma curled up to his chest, her hand gripping his shirt so it tugged at the neckline. Her humid breath puffed over the skin exposed there, and a part of him eased. She was here, with him. They were both safe. All was right with his world.

Beeyun was careful as he traversed the halls, not wanting to bump Emma into the walls or doorways. He paid no attention to the others. He only registered Emma's friend Lacy in passing before fleeing to the control room, their territory. Crossing straight to their bed, he leaned over to place her in it.

"No, wait, Beeyun."

He froze, looking down at her. She'd been so quiet and still on the way there, he'd thought she might have fallen asleep. "Yes?"

She made moves to get out of his arms, but he held tighter. She huffed. "I have to get to the console. I need to set things back to rights."

Beeyun eased her legs to the floor, but didn't let go, following her to the console he'd become increasingly familiar with. He puffed up with pride when he recognized what she was doing. He was actually learning these things.

I can do this.

I can live in their world.

A hum started up, the life support pumping air through the vents once more. It was still cold, though, and now the circulating air just made him feel colder as the sweat chilled against his skin. He rubbed his forearms, holding Emma tighter, hoping to keep her a little warmer.

She yawned again, reaching for her mouth.

"Come on," he said, pulling her backward. "You need sleep."

"But…"

"No buts. Sleep." He dragged her with him and laid her down on their bed, wrapping blankets tight around her small body to ensure she didn't catch a chill. For good measure, he curled himself around her, using his own body heat to keep her warm.

Beeyun sighed and closed his eyes. He wasn't tired physically, but the day had certainly taken its toll on them all mentally. He needed this. There was a certain serenity, a peace, to this pose. His body relaxed for the first time in hours, leaving him a little sore but relieved. It was over. They were safe. There was nothing else to worry about.

And with that thought top on his mind, he drifted off to sleep.

<hr />

Everyone else had returned to their rooms hours ago, but West simply couldn't be still. He was exhausted, in pain, but still on edge, still waiting for the other shoe to drop. It didn't feel like it was over. He kept expecting something else to go wrong, something else to happen.

West shivered. In spite of his constant movement, he was developing a chill. He should have taken a shower, but that felt too vulnerable. A layer of sweat chilled him to his core in the cool air blasting from the vents.

What does she have this system set on? Artic tundra?

He stormed off, limping to the control room, determined to get her to turn up the heat. Along the way, people peeped out of their rooms, questioning looks in their eyes. Each one shivered, cold and afraid, asking him without words if it was over. He didn't say anything. He didn't want to promise if he couldn't deliver. They'd been through too much already.

West reached the control room, which was unlocked. He pushed the door open. Emma and the alien lay on a mattress on the floor, Emma wrapped in blankets and her alien. They looked like a couple, and for the first time, he didn't just see the man as "other" but as a man, caring for his woman.

Beeyun lifted his head and shook it, indicating West should remain quiet. West paused. He'd seen the bodies of the creatures this man had killed, knew he'd done a great deal to help them, providing information and expertise, protecting West's people when he could not. "Heat," he whispered, trying to be as quiet as possible.

The other man nodded and mumbled, "She must have forgot," under his breath. Standing up, Beeyun walked over to the console and typed in a series of numbers. A new hum filled the ship, and he knew the engines had started up.

Ignition codes?! When the hell had the alien learned the ignition codes for the ship? His blood ran cold for a moment, and he completely forgot the gratitude he'd felt only moments before. West crooked his finger at the alien and jerked his head toward the door. The other man only nodded, following him out.

When the control room door closed, he ripped into him. "How the hell do *you* know the ignition codes for *my* ship?"

He merely shrugged. "Emma taught me."

"Emma *taught* you?" West stared at the man, baffled, not able to compute that this alien, this primitive, had been *taught* an essential function of his ship. With the ignition codes, this alien could *steal* his ship, not that West would let him.

Beeyun nodded. "Yes. Since we would be shutting off the engines, she wanted to ensure they could be turned on again should she be incapacitated." He cringed. "Your people would not survive long enough for a rescue without them. They would eventually succumb to the cold."

West paused, accepting the logic of giving a second person the codes. "But why you? You're not a member of this crew."

The bigger man only shrugged, then tensed and looked over his shoulder before quickly opening the control room door and running to his woman's side. As soon as the door opened, West heard what had alarmed him. Emma was crying out in her sleep.

He turned around and walked away, making sure the door closed to give them privacy. This was not his domain, and he would leave them be, even if he very much wanted to chew Emma out right now.

"Tsu," Beeyun said against her ear as he slipped into their bed behind her.

Emma buried her head against his chest, afraid to close her eyes. Her heart raced, and she shivered as the nightmare faded. She'd dreamed they hadn't killed all the creatures, that they had returned, this time slipping into the control room in their sleep and trying to eat them alive. They bit at her, taking chunks out of her flesh as she tried to wake Beeyun, but he wouldn't respond.

She breathed in his scent, some indefinable allure that settled her rattled nerves.

"It's okay. I have you. I will protect you, keep you safe. You never need fear." Beeyun continued on, holding her tight in his arms, petting her hair and unleashing an unending litany of soothing words.

"I'm afraid to sleep," she finally said into his chest.

"You need your rest, my brave one. You are exhausted."

She was. She could feel her heavy, gritty eyes, her sluggish body. But she couldn't shake her fear. What if they hadn't got them all? What if they came back? Would they be prepared? Could they truly stop them?

"I will watch over you, protect your sleep."

She looked up at him, smirked a little. "You can't protect me from nightmares."

"No, but I can soothe you afterwards."

She nodded, but her tired eyes wouldn't close. She relaxed into him, taking comfort from his presence, his warmth. Maybe that would be enough to help her sleep.

Eventually.

***

Emma woke with a start to an automated voice. "Ecological Quarantine has now been lifted."

Her eyes drifted closed once more, and she smiled into Beeyun's chest, feeling a little secure again. They were safe. The pests were gone. They'd killed them all. She could sleep.

Finally.

CHAPTER TWENTY-NINE

mma stepped from the control room the next morning feeling refreshed, almost back to normal. The aftermath of the events still haunted her, like a shadow over her mind, but it would fade with time. Meanwhile, she desperately needed a shower. Her skin felt sticky and clammy. Her hair was a greasy, matted mess. She wasn't fit to be seen, or smelled, by anyone right now.

So, of course, West stepped into her path, glaring down at her.

She waited for it, wondering if her body odor was wafting to him.

"You gave an *alien* my ship's ignition codes? Are you insane? I should write you up for this."

"An alien? His name is Beeyun. And he's done nothing but save your ass."

"Save our asses? When the hell did he save our asses?"

"Oh, I don't know." She rolled her eyes, then pointed her finger in his face. "Maybe when he tried to scare us away from the giant field of psychotropic pollen? Or when he convinced his brother not to kill you all and let you leave? Or how about when he fought off the creatures that invaded the engine room?" Okay, maybe convincing his brother was more Emma than Beeyun, but the captain didn't need to know that.

"Enough!" Lacy said, out of breath from running up to them. "You two are like children." She looked back and forth between them, shocked at their behavior.

Emma felt a little sheepish at the chastisement, but Captain West just glared, clearly unhappy with the dressing down from someone who wasn't a superior.

He turned to Emma. "You've been warned. He is not a member of this crew and should *not* have access to sensitive information." He walked away.

Emma shook her head. What other choice was there? They'd all had roles to play. At the time, it was the most logical solution, wasn't it?

"He *is* the captain, ya' know," Lacy said, dragging her out of her thoughts.

"Well, he's still an ass."

"That too," Lacy said, smirking at her. "Come on. Let's get something to eat."

***

Emma didn't see West again for the rest of the flight, which was probably for the best. She mostly kept to the control room, cuddling with Beeyun. But he wasn't always there, at least mentally. He seemed tense, distracted even though everything was going smoothly. Not a single system had gone down since they'd killed off all the creatures.

"What's wrong?" she said, reaching up to caress the side of his face. The color difference distracted her, made her smile, and she couldn't help continuing. It was like an addiction.

"Nothing," he said. Even so, the distraction remained on his features.

She tilted his face to look at her, not satisfied with his answer. "Bullshit."

He frowned, focusing on her again, finally. "What's bullshit? I know shit means excrement, but I'm not sure why you would reference that now."

Emma snorted, loving the moment. "Bullshit is a word used when we don't believe what someone has said. It's vulgar, but it's basically calling what the person just said the verbal equivalent of bullshit."

"Meaning excrement." He nodded, thoughtful.

"Which means you're not telling me the truth."

He scoffed. "I would never lie to you, my Emma."

"Beeyun, not telling me what you're feeling, what is worrying you, when I specifically ask, insisting it is nothing, *is* lying. If you said you didn't want to discuss it, that wouldn't be lying. But I know something's going on in that head of yours." She tapped his temple with a fingertip. "Let me in."

Beeyun didn't speak for a long moment. He didn't look at her either, but she didn't worry about that. He needed to work it out himself, and she would happily wait for him.

"I'm concerned," he said finally.

"About?" This was like pulling teeth. It seemed some things were universal. Men just didn't like to discuss their emotions.

"About Earth. About the reception I'll receive. Humans have not been the most welcoming."

She smirked. "Well, you did kind of wreck our efforts for a while there. That and running us off your planet are bound to create some frustrations and hostilities."

"And why wouldn't the same hold true on Earth?"

"Because, you're not there to wreck anything. You're there to foster relations between your people and mine. Trust me, the type of people who choose that profession are much more open minded. And they have no reason to be hostile. You've done nothing to them."

"I suppose."

"You know, humans have had interactions with aliens before. We have treaties with several species. I won't deny that not every person on Earth trusts aliens, but those in power understand their uses, and that's probably the important part.

"Everything's going to be fine."

Emma jerked awake when static, and then a voice, came through the radio. "Vessel, please identify yourself and state your purpose."

She jumped to her feet, dropping into her chair and activating the comm. "This is the USS *Endeavour* requesting permission to dock."

The radio was silent for several moments, probably so the man could verify her information. "USS *Endeavour*, you are not due to return. Please state your purpose."

"We encountered issues with our mission, which was deemed a lost cause."

And then she wondered if she'd told the captain why Beeyun had joined them. Obviously, Earth didn't know they were returning, so they definitely didn't know Beeyun was joining them. Should she say? Then maybe some delegates could meet them at the dock. It couldn't hurt, right? "We are arriving with a foreign ambassador."

"Proceed," the voice said, and the radio clicked off.

Emma shrugged and prepared for docking. In front of her, the Earth loomed like a blueberry covered in frost. After a few more moments, the big, metal monstrosity in the shape of a bicycle wheel came into view. All interstellar ships had to stop at the space station first. A lot of ships had permanent dock assignments here.

Their ship didn't, so they pulled into one of the guest docking stations. Each spoke could accept multiple ships, the number of ships depended on the ship size it was designed to accommodate. She turned on her docking camera, which gave a view of the docking door and port with a digital overlay helping her identify if she was lined up properly.

Once aligned, she activated a command, and the seal engaged, locking the *Endeavour* to the space station. She opened up the intercom, "We've finalized docking and everyone may disembark."

The *Endeavour* was big, small enough to enter atmosphere, but too big for most landing sites on Earth. It had been built in space and would remain there. The passengers and crew would take shuttles down to Earth. This was more convenient, anyway. They were all from different places, and there were far more landing sites for shuttles than ships.

"Come on, Beeyun," she said, reaching out her hand.

He grasped it a little too tightly, but she just squeezed back, not saying a word about his unease. With her other hand, she grabbed her bags and walked to the exit.

Outside, a group of people in NASA and NSS uniforms waited to welcome them, which she found strange. Those two organizations *ran* all space programs in the United States, including the one she'd been piloting, but there should have been a plainclothes ambassador among them, right? Emma stepped up to them and let go of Beeyun's hand to salute.

She pointed at Beeyun, "This is Beeyun of HD 85512 b. He has come with us to open relations between our two species."

They nodded to Beeyun, and Emma noticed the surprise on their faces. What were they surprised by?

"Come with us," the leader of the group said before turning toward the exit.

Around them, the passengers and crew split off, some heading toward the guest bunks on the space station while others supervised the unloading of their personal belongings and equipment.

She took Beeyun's hand again and followed the group to a conference room, where the leader turned and stared at their hands clasped together. He frowned, but held his tongue and ushered them into the room.

The room was like any conference room. A long telecom table with chairs around it took up the middle of the room. A buffet to the right held a refreshment station, and a presentation display covered the back wall.

She sighed and sat down at the table, drumming her fingers.

Time passed, and no one showed. Emma stood up and started to pace, to worry. Something was wrong. Something just didn't feel right.

But she didn't say anything, not wanting to worry Beeyun, who had already shown signs of nerves long before this. He was relying on her to help him navigate this situation, and she refused to let him down.

But what was taking them so long?

Beeyun watched Emma with amusement. She had taken to pacing the small room, worry stiffening her frame. She was obviously concerned, disturbed, though she insisted it would be fine. He suspected she didn't believe it, but he chose to listen to her assessment from earlier, not this anxiety she expressed now.

The moments dragged on, and the display on the far wall held an image that seemed to mark time. A full count of sixty had passed since they were ushered into the room. Then the door slipped open, letting in a small man wearing different garments from the others who led them to this room.

He stood, nodding at the man. "Hello, I am Beeyun."

The man froze in place, a look of shock on his pale face. "Please, sit," he said, composing himself. He took the seat opposite Beeyun.

Emma stepped in behind Beeyun, hovering at his shoulder, lending him support.

Silence filled the room. Beeyun knew nothing about his new role, didn't know what to say, how to start. The silence grew, becoming awkward, and he resisted the urge to shift in his seat. He wasn't the type to sit idly, and he would have felt more comfortable *doing* something, but what? He suspected his new role would never be an active one.

"Are you new to this?" he finally asked, not knowing what else to say.

The other man let out a humorless laugh. "Actually, I've never been involved in first encounters before."

"What does that mean?"

He shrugged. "Well, I've always worked with already established alien allies, not new species."

"And who would normally be here?"

"People more adventurous than me," the man mumbled under his breath, not realizing Beeyun could hear him.

Beeyun smiled, seeing a more lively side to the man now. He thought about commenting on the man's words, but decided it would be counterproductive, possibly making the situation even more awkward.

Time passed slowly at first, as they each warmed up to each other, not knowing what to say, how to proceed. It made Beeyun feel better, more comfortable. He wasn't alone in this. He wasn't the only one who didn't know what they were doing.

Over time, Beeyun told him about his people, about their planet with its purple vegetation, creatures with anywhere from 4 to 8 limbs, how their people once lived on four separate continents but were reunited by a shifting of the continents. He told about their four original languages, how they had united their four tribes by creating a new language inspired by all four.

He told him about their dedication to maintaining their world's natural state, about the many dangerous but often magnificent wonders the planet had to offer. He told him how they used the reusable natural resources to their advantage, using what the world already provided.

The ambassador told him in kind about Earth, about its many people, all of them different, unique. He told of their many technologies, advances, space travel. He told of their alliances with many other alien species. It was both disturbing and fascinating. Humans managed to simultaneously abuse and try to protect their planet, as if they couldn't make up their mind on what was important.

He suspected their many cultures might be part of the problem. With hundreds of cultures, it would be nearly impossible to settle on a single course of action. He suspected, for that reason, some humans would not be hakkan, would be able to live on his planet without upsetting the natural balance.

"I believe our people would be willing to host humans on our planet, assuming those humans follow our laws and cultural dictates." He glared for emphasis, leaning over the table. "But don't forget, our people are perfectly capable of defending ourselves, even if we do not have ships capable of traveling the stars."

"Excellent," the ambassador said, reaching his hand out.

Beeyun looked at it, unsure about the gesture.

Emma chuckled near his ear. "Grip it and shake gently."

He nodded and did so.

The ambassador let go and stood up. "We can discuss those possibilities more at our next meeting. Considering your planet's unique attributes and your culture, I'm sure, at the least, there will be plenty of scientists willing to conform to your requirements."

Beeyun nodded.

"Come. I'll show you to your quarters."

They followed him, Emma taking Beeyun's hand once again.
It felt like a beginning.

"Why was I not affected by the maenu?" Emma mused aloud. It had been a few days since they arrived at the space station. Talks with ambassadors had gone well so far, but Beeyun wasn't allowed on Earth, which was normal. The space station and moon station were considered neutral ground, even if they were used as military bases as well. She turned to Beeyun, who sat reclined on the couch, amusement he would pay for later twinkling in his eyes. "Is that normal?"

"I've never heard of it before," he said, seriousness slipping into his expression.

And yet Lacy and her family hadn't been affected either. Everyone else had.

"I'm going to go see Lacy," she said, absently leaving the room.

Most of the crew and passengers of the *Endeavour* were still on the space station. Since they hadn't been expected, there weren't enough shuttles to take them to Earth. Add to that, they'd planned on being gone a good while, so most of them didn't have a place to stay.

She walked the halls, a question high in her mind. It nagged at her, the little puzzle pieces starting to fit together with alarming ease.

Not being affected by the maenu even when everyone around her had been.

How she'd often been able to reach down for reserves of speed and endurance when she felt motivated. When the explosion happened, she'd run as fast as she could, outstripping everyone else who reacted. She'd left them in the dust, forgetting about them entirely until they caught up on the way back.

How she always recovered from illnesses and injuries quicker than most. She'd almost completely healed from those cuts from the wire by the next morning. Hell, she'd hurt herself more times than she could count on this mission—hitting her head, dropping sheet metal on her foot, burning her hand, hammering her fingers—but she always forgot about it within a day or two. Was that normal? She'd always healed that quickly, but maybe it wasn't…

Then there was the fact that she was home schooled and thus never underwent the standardized testing back during the big scare.

She reached Lacy's door and knocked. After a moment, the door slipped open, and the words blurted out of her. "Are you a shifter?"

Lacy's stance pulled back at the sudden question, but then she recovered, a small smile on her face. "Yeah, so?"

Emma walked away in a daze.

"Emma?" a voice said behind her, fading into nothingness.

I'm a shifter.

The thought rang through Emma's head, a fact that should have been obvious long ago, but she had pushed it away. When she was a kid, it was too dangerous to even consider the possibility. After all, shifters ended up in camps, even children. She remembered she used to have nightmares about it. Her mother would reassure her by saying, "I would never let you end up there."

It had soothed her, but she'd never once considered maybe her mother knew more than she said, that maybe they were shifters. She'd never said anything. Had her mother known? Why hadn't she said?

I'm a shifter.

She'd never had a flamboyant change like some shifters, though she supposed she could if she tried, if she focused. She'd never changed into an animal or tried to change into another person. The future stretched before her, forever changed and a little terrifying.

Looking up, she found herself outside the suite she shared with Beeyun. The door slipped open at her command. Beeyun sat there, a quizzical look on his face.

"Emma? Is everything all right?" He stood, reaching out to her.

"I think I'm a shifter. I think that's why the maenu didn't affect me."

"What is a shifter?" He moved forward, wrapping her in his arms, rubbing her back.

Emma relaxed into the embrace. It felt good to be held by him, and she could just fall asleep right there. "A shifter, shape-shifter, is a species on Earth, although species might be a misnomer. They reproduce readily with humans. They have significant control over their bodies, even to the point of changing their appearance.”

He brushed back her hair with one hand, looking into her eyes. “Changing their appearance?” His face lit up. “Your eyes.”

She pulled back slightly. “What about my eyes?”

“Well, I had noticed sometimes they looked a little different. Different colors, I guess. It’s subtle. I didn’t think anything of it, figured it was a quirk of your biology.”

She reached up to her cheek, touching just below her left eye. How had no one ever noticed that before? When did it happen? *Why* did it happen? Her jaw fell open, the reality sinking in.

I’m a shifter.

But what did it really mean for her? Shifters were mostly accepted now. Discriminated against, but accepted. Certainly, the camps had been shut down for over a decade.

“What does this mean?” Beeyun said, interrupting her thoughts.

Emma pulled back, opening her mouth, but nothing came out at first. What *did* this mean? She didn’t know, but she suspected things wouldn’t have gone the way they had if she hadn’t been a shifter. If she’d been a normal human, she would have been affected by the maenu. Maybe Beeyun wouldn’t have saved her. Maybe he wouldn’t be looking at her like she hung the moon right now. She ran a finger along the side of his face, the fear starting to slip away.

She shrugged, her lip curling up impishly. “I’m not sure, but I do know one thing.” She leaned in.

“What’s that?”

She kissed him and pulled back. "It brought us together."

"It did?"

"Oh yes." She leaned in, kissing his cheek this time before pulling back again. "And I wouldn't have it any other way."

"Neither would I."

READY FOR MORE?

This series will continue with Ellie, the daughter of Emma and Beeyun, in Shifting Cargo.

Ellie, a cargo ship captain, needs to land her ship for repairs, only shortly after landing, an alien soldier tries to commandeer her ship…

Now Available for Pre-Order

I love building relationships with my readers. As part of that, I regularly send emails with deleted scenes, never before seen excerpts, pre-order and new release announcements, and more.

If you sign up to receive these emails, I'll send you <u>Mila's Flight</u>, the prequel to the Darkest Day series, FREE.

Join Now to Get Your Free Ebook

www.theeternalscribe.com

DID YOU ENJOY THE BOOK?

Reviews are among the most important tools in my arsenal for getting my books in front of readers like yourself. I'm just one person. No matter how much I shout, my voice can only carry so far.

But do you want to know what does carry?

A crowd.

When one voice joins another who joins another, that matters. *That* gets heard.

Let your own voice be heard by leaving an honest review. It only takes a few minutes, but makes a major difference not just to me as an author, but to readers like yourself who are trying to decide on their next read.

Thanks again!

Danielle

ACKNOWLEDGMENTS

A special thanks to the following members of my mailing list for helping this book be the best it could be...

colcam
Maria K.
Karen S.
Kort P.
Robin B.-G.
Tammy W.
Kris S.
Evie F.
Irene O'B.
geosun_2000
Darrell N.
Maria E.
Chris J.

ABOUT THE AUTHOR

Danielle Forrest is a Paranormal SciFi author and Medical Laboratory Scientist based out of Indianapolis, IN.

She has dedicated her life so far to two things:

Science & Books

So it really shouldn't be a surprise if science finds its way into even the most fantastical examples of her writing.

Sign up for her mailing list at www.theeternalscribe.com to get access to exclusive content and updates.

facebook.com/theeternalscribe

twitter.com/theternalscribe

instagram.com/theeternalscribe

goodreads.com/theeternalscr_be

amazon.com/author/danielleforrest

bookbub.com/profile/danielle-forrest

ALSO BY DANIELLE FORREST

THE DARKEST DAY SERIES

Mila's Flight

When she shifts for the first time, an unsuspecting shape-shifter runs away to live on the streets. But after a mysterious man enters her life violently, she'll die if she doesn't stop running from her problems.

Mila's Shift

Hiding from a government bent on eradicating her kind, a paranoid shape-shifter steals her dead friend's identity to board a military spaceship, but when the captain discovers her secret, she must learn to trust again or no one will survive.

Tristan's Choice

After he receives orders for a new mission, an unambitious space ship captain transports diplomats to the moon for a historic treaty negotiation with an alien race. But when an alien ship attacks, interrupting the talks, he must warn Earth or everyone will die.

Terra's Fate

When a child in her care shifts for the first time, a prejudiced shape-shifter in denial must escape the shifter camp imprisoning them both. But when an alien invasion looms, threatening what little peace she's found, she must accept herself or lose everyone everything.

The Darkest Day Collection

Includes Mila's Shift, Tristan's Choice, Terra's Fate, and a bonus novella, May's Nightmare.